Ponies in the Blizzard

A wild beast is loose near Park Farm Animal Centre. The beast has not been seen close to, but the police suspect that it is none other than Kelly, the Wells family's beloved watchdog. However, the children are certain that Kelly is not involved. Determined to seek out the beast and to clear Kelly's name, they become lost in a blizzard. Can they survive the elements and catch the beast?

Christine Pullein-Thompson has been involved with horses all her life – she opened a riding school with her sisters when she was fourteen. Again with her sisters, Josephine and Diana, she has written *Black Beauty's Family* 1 and 2, published by Beaver. This is her third book about the Wells family – the others are *Ponies in the Park* and *Ponies in the Forest*.

Also in Beaver by Christine Pullein-Thompson

PONIES
IN THE
BLIZZARD

Christine Pullein-Thompson

Beaver Books

A Beaver Original
Published by Arrow Books Limited
17–21 Conway Street, London W1P 6JD
An imprint of the Hutchinson Publishing Group
London Melbourne Sydney Auckland
Johannesburg and agencies throughout the world

First published 1984
Copyright ©Christine Pullein-Thompson 1984

Set in Linoterm Baskerville by
JH Graphics Limited, Reading

Printed and bound in Great Britain by
Anchor Brendon Limited, Tiptree, Essex

ISBN 0 09 938060 9

CONTENTS

1

We must do something

It was winter; the coldest winter for years. The
trees and hedges looked as though they were
decorated with Christmas tinsel. The duck pond at
Park Farm Animal Centre was frozen over. The
Wells family were sitting in their old-fashioned
kitchen talking about the beast which was terroris-
ing the area.

'They think it lives in the osiers by the river;
they even think it goes under the water; they're
turning it into a Loch Ness monster,' explained
Dad laughing.

'It's a good story,' Mum said.

Rosie always thought that this was the best
moment of the day, when the mucking-out and
feeding were done and they all sat near the
Raeburn drinking coffee. Rosie, square-faced, grey-
eyed, was the down-to-earth one in the family. The
one who could calm a nervous pony with a few
words, who wanted to make horses her career.
Clara was more dramatic, more interested in her

appearance. She saw herself on the stage, or on television, famous as an actress. Andy was somewhere between the two; long and lean like Clara, he was more strung up than either of them though he rarely showed it. He worried over money and because his mother worked too hard. Often he felt as tense as a horse before a race. His dream was to make a fortune.

'The river is miles away, Dad,' he said. 'So why are we worrying?'

'We are not worrying,' Dad said, swilling his mug in the sink. 'We are just talking about the beast. Personally I think it's half dog, half cat.'

'I think it's a puma,' said Mum.

'Do you think it kills horses?' asked Rosie.

'It hasn't yet. But there's always a first time.'

'I think it's exciting. I think we should hunt it,' said Clara. 'Then if we catch it, we will be famous.'

'For twenty-four hours, then forgotten,' said down-to-earth Rosie.

'It would be a good beginning to a New Year,' insisted Clara. 'Are we doing anything on New Year's Eve? It's tomorrow.'

The others had forgotten. It was like Clara to remember. Rosie had been worrying about the animals, about the guinea pigs who always looked so cold and the ponies who were under-exercised.

Andy had been worrying about not having enough new animals to bring in the crowds when they opened on Easter Monday.

'You must make resolutions,' said Mum. 'Andy must stop biting his nails; Clara, you can help more with the washing up; and, Rosie, you must stop being a martyr. You don't have to do all the work while the others stay inside.'

'But I like it,' said Rosie, which was true.

But all that was before the policemen came. They were in the kitchen again then, enjoying tea. Buttering home-made scones with home-made butter, piling on home-made jam, talking about the weather because Dad had just heard the forecast which promised snow. There was a kitten sitting on Rosie's knee and Kelly the big guard dog was lying at Dad's feet. The horses had been settled for the night, Marigold the Jersey cow milked; the donkeys were wearing the rugs Mum had made for them; the fancy bantams – silkies, frizzles and Japanese bantams – were on their perches; the sheep were deep in straw; the two black pigs asleep together; the goats eating the nettle hay made for them earlier in the year. The year which was coming to an end they had called 'make or break' year – and they had survived. It looked as though it would be like any other winter; yet it was to be one they would never forget.

'Listen, there's a car stopping. Who the devil can that be?' exclaimed Dad. He stood to listen – tallish, fair haired, bronzed by the weather.

'It can't be the electricity man because he came last week,' Mum said, going to the window, drawing

9

back the thick blue curtains, peering into the winter dark. 'Oh my God, it's a police car . . .'

'So what?' answered Dad. 'We haven't done anything wrong.' He walked towards the door still in his socks, while the three children looked at one another and said nothing.

'Good evening, sir.' Two policemen stepped inside, taking off their caps and rubbing their hands together. 'What a night . . .' Mum said, 'Tea?' and went automatically to the teapot, while Andy felt his guts tighten and Clara thought that both policemen were young and handsome and Rosie asked herself, 'What have we done wrong?'

'We're just making a few enquiries,' said the older policeman, who had a small pencil moustache. 'I understand you keep some wild animals here . . .'

He was looking at David Wells. 'Not wild, just domesticated.'

'No bears from Asia? Or pumas or big cats? No wolves?'

'No. Nothing exciting. We are not a zoo, just a little animal centre for families to visit. We have pony rides and a pet's corner, that sort of thing. I haven't got a licence to keep wild animals; you must know that . . .' Dad sounded defensive which made the knot tighten in Andy's stomach.

'What about the big fella?' The policeman with the moustache bent down to look at Kelly, who had not even barked but looked as guilty as the rest of the Wells family though they had nothing to be guilty about.

'What about him? He's quite harmless,' said Bronwen Wells. 'He's like a big baby. A real old slob.' She bent down to stroke Kelly who had a head like a Great Dane, ears like a Boxer dog and the tail of a rough Collie – a mongrel in the truest sense of the word.

'He's our guard dog; that's why he's here, but he wouldn't hurt a fly,' said Dad. 'Our place was broken up last summer, animals were killed; that's why we got him.'

The other policeman took a photograph from his wallet and passed it round. Rosie looked at the animal in the photograph and her legs felt so weak she had to sit down, while Andy turned pale and Clara cried, 'It looks like Kelly, but it isn't him. His ears are different and his nose is wider . . .'

'And his paws are larger,' said Andy in a tight voice.

'No one is accusing Kelly; they are just making routine enquiries,' said Dad.

'That's right. We just want to know where your dog was last night,' said the policeman with the moustache whom Rosie had dubbed 'the nasty one'.

'Here, in here, he sleeps in the house,' Dad was emphatic. Rosie knew differently but was too afraid to confess that she had let Kelly out at two A.M. and had forgotten all about him until dawn when she

11

heard his whining by the back door. She wanted to speak, but the words stuck in her throat, while the two policemen stood up saying, 'Thanks for the tea. May we have a look around?'

Dad nodded, fetched a coat, a torch, put some sugar knobs in his pocket. He looked tired as they went out through the back door, letting in a sudden rush of cold air.

'Whew! I liked the younger one, the one without the moustache,' exclaimed Clara.

'They are accusing Kelly, aren't they?' cried Andy.

'No, not yet anyway,' said Mum.

Rosie was trying to speak, trying to confess.

Clara went on talking. 'Perhaps we'll see the beast; perhaps he'll come here—'

'Kelly *was* out last night. I let him out,' Rosie said with tears falling down her cheeks. 'He kept asking.'

'For how long?' Mum was pouring herself another cup of tea, her knuckles white against the teapot.

'I don't know. It was so cold. I went back to bed. I fell asleep. I didn't mean to. Then I heard him howling. I didn't look at the clock, but the cocks were crowing . . .'

'Oh my God!' said Bronwen.

'You should have said. You told a lie,' said Clara.

'Shut up,' shouted Andy. 'You don't care

12

about Kelly. All you care about is the policeman.'

'Was he alright when he came in? I mean, did he
have blood on him?' asked Mum.

'I don't know. I didn't look. Oh Mum, I am
sorry.'

'It wasn't your fault.'

'If only I hadn't gone back to sleep . . .'

'He hasn't been proved guilty. The killing has
been going on for some time.'

'And he's been going out for some time,' said
Rosie, tears streaming down her cheeks.

'You mean—' began Mum.

'Yes.'

Suddenly there was silence. Rosie could hear the
clock ticking and the new young logs hissing as they
burnt in the Raeburn, and Kelly's breathing . . .

'How many times?'

'Only twice.'

'That isn't so bad, then,' said Mum, trying to
look on the bright side (as she always did, thought
Rosie miserably).

'Nothing has been proved,' insisted Andy.

Dad was coming back saying, 'Goodnight. Thank
you for calling. We'll keep in touch.'

Outside the moon had risen turning everything to
silver. The door opened and let in the moonlight;
then shut it out again.

'They were only doing their duty, don't look so
fraught,' said Dad taking off his coat.

'Kelly was out last night, David,' Mum said.

'Why didn't you say?' Dad had not moved. He looked rooted.

'Rosie knew—'

'You mean you let him out, and didn't say so?'

She nodded miserably.

'Go to bed, get out of my sight. You were dishonest. You lied to the police,' shouted Dad.

'No she didn't, Dad. She didn't speak. They didn't ask her. You don't know the law, Dad,' shouted Andy.

'I had better ring up the police straight away,' said Dad, looking for the telephone directory.

'If he was a killer, he would have killed some of our animals; don't be silly, Dad,' shouted Clara.

'He hasn't been proved guilty,' said Rosie. She stayed in the kitchen, knowing that her father's temper would subside in a matter of minutes, that she would not be punished in spite of the awfulness of what she had done.

'I think we are all being rather silly,' said Mum, taking the directory away from Dad. 'There is no evidence against poor old Kelly, is there?'

'Only that two sheep were killed last night at Heron's farm which is only about three kilometres from here,' said Dad, flopping down into a chair.

'But he hasn't been proved guilty,' said Rosie, 'and you've said yourself that he's the gentlest dog you've ever known. When you brought him home you said he would never kill a burglar, because he had a gun dog's mouth. Your memory is very short, Dad. His teeth can't have changed.'

'And now he's a killer, all in the space of a few days,' said Clara.

'I am not an expert,' said Dad slowly. 'But I know one thing – that big slob of a dog will now be chained day and night. No one is to let him out. He is never to go off the lead. He will be solely my responsibility.'

'You are condemning him to prison before he's even been proved guilty,' cried Clara angrily.

'It's the only sensible thing to do,' replied Mum. 'We must do it. There is no other way.'

And all the time that big slob of a dog was shut in the scullery, sitting in an enormous basket, his huge jaws resting on the side of it, his eyes mournful, his ears listening. When he wagged his tail the whole basket shook.

'We've got to do something,' said Rosie later. She knelt beside Kelly, her eyes brimming with tears.

The animal centre was shut for the winter. The old walled garden was nearly bare of vegetables. The young animals were growing stronger and more were being acquired all the time. The Victorian kitchen museum was being improved with new exhibits found in sales and antique shops. The tack

15

was clean in the tack room, the harness shining, the carts newly painted. Christmas was only just over; a new year about to begin. And they all had plans for the New Year: Rosie wanted to ride her first dressage test; Andy planned to become a gymkhana champion; Clara was saving up to have her hair permed. Dad had decided to cultivate rare plants in the walled garden. Mum wanted to open a luncheon bar.

'We must do something,' repeated Rosie.

But it was not until the next day that they decided what to do. And it was afternoon before Andy said, 'I think we should look for the beast ourselves, go out on the ponies, prove Kelly innocent. No one else will. It's up to us.'

They had all slept badly; the morning had dragged. Mum looked exhausted; Dad had spent the hours struggling with ground elder in the walled garden; and one of the Muscovy ducks had died in the night for no apparent reason. Above, the sky seemed to promise nothing but snow; the whole countryside appeared to be waiting for it. Afterwards Mum was to say, 'If only I hadn't been so tired, I would have stopped them going. If only I wasn't always so tired . . .'

And Dad was to curse them, to say, 'They take after your side of the family, Bronwen; not one of them has an ounce of common sense.' But that was to be later, much, much later.

Now suddenly the three children were filled with excitement.

'I'll take my camera,' cried Andy.

'Here comes Emma,' shrieked Rosie.

'We need a gun,' cried Clara.

'We'll take riding whips,' said Andy.

'Emma, we're going after the beast. Hurry,' shouted Rosie.

'I'll take my penknife, money, string,' Andy muttered.

'We'll be famous,' cried Clara.

And Emma stood waving, calling, 'What is it now?' thinking, they are all mad ... stark, staring ...

'We're going to find the beast, you know, *the beast*,' shouted Rosie. And now Emma was running too, while all around the trees were bare, the hedges brown, the grass turning to mud. And the sky was darkening, so that suddenly night seemed quite near, though actually it was only ten minutes to two o'clock.

Then they stood making plans, Emma with her hair tied back behind her ears, wearing old jeans and a polo-necked sweater. She looked like a model, which was something Clara envied beyond words.

'We are going after the beast, because the police are accusing Kelly. There's no time to lose because soon it will be dark,' Rosie explained.

'Exactly,' said Emma in her matter-of-fact voice. 'And you know it's going to snow later.'

'I've got a camera. I'm going to collect evidence,' cried Andy, running for a saddle.

'And we're going to be famous,' said Clara with certainty. As though it was preordained, thought Emma, following her towards the tack room, her hands already freezing in her expensive yellow riding gloves.

2

'Where are the others?'

'Where are we going?' asked Emma, with a snaffle bridle over her arm.

'To Heron's farm,' said Rosie.

'Sheep were killed there yesterday,' added Andy, bridling small grey Caspar who only he was light enough to ride.

Emma kept her pony, a Connemara called Sandpiper, with theirs at the Animal Centre. She lived with her father in a new house on the estate beyond the walled garden, and was older than them, and old for her years.

'It's going to snow. You know that, don't you?' she asked now. ·

'We are not going far,' answered Rosie.

'Only there and back,' said Andy.

'We must clear Kelly's name,' explained Clara, slipping a bit between black Bramble's teeth, while Rosie led dun Highland Lapwing out into the yard. Another minute and they were mounted, riding out of the yard.

'Don't be long,' called Bronwen, as they rode past the farmhouse, which was low and ancient with beams and lattice windows and thick old doors, a house they loved and would always love . . . a house which had once belonged to Bronwen's uncle and had been left to her when he died.

Behind them Dad was already settling the other animals for the night, talking to the pygmy goats as though they were children, putting the donkeys to bed. Another hour and Mum would be milking and then the electric lights would be on in the old-fashioned yard, shining out into the night like beacons.

Suddenly Rosie was happy. We are doing something useful, she thought, maybe saving animals from being killed. We are not wasting time. Rosie had a horror of wasting time – while Clara could sit all afternoon doing nothing Rosie had to be occupied. Dad called it a kind of disease while Mum said she was just a compulsive worker, and that she would never be cured now.

'It's getting warmer,' said Andy, his feet near Caspar's knees, his camera bumping up and down on his back.

'It always does before it snows,' answered Emma gloomily. 'I think you are idiots. I am not staying out long.'

'We are only going to Heron's farm,' argued Rosie. 'It won't take us more than half an hour.'

They trotted briskly down a bridleway, splashing

through mud, a light wind cold on their faces, the sky still ominous, everything suddenly silent. And Emma knew that silence, recognised it as the silence before the storm. Her spine started to tingle, and she felt her insides tighten with anxiety.

'I think you are mad. What good can we do?' she asked.

'Don't get fussed; we are only going as far as the farm. We just want to tell Mr Hayward that it was not Kelly who killed his sheep,' replied Rosie, urging Lapwing on.

'The police are accusing Kelly,' Clara explained. 'And you know what that means . . .'

'What?'

'That he'll be shot sooner or later, that's what it means,' shouted Andy, trailing behind on little grey Caspar.

'No it doesn't mean that! The police are not like that.'

'Yes they are.'

They could see the farmhouse now, grey stone, with white framed windows, with fruit trees in the front and yards behind full of cattle. The ponies were reluctant to hurry, particularly Lapwing, and the wind blew straight into the children's faces.

Reaching the farm, the others insisted that Rosie should go to the front door.

'You are the most tactful,' Emma said.

'And good with farmers,' added Andy.

'I always say the wrong thing,' said Clara,

21

patting Bramble's neck which still had the marks left on it from last year's sweet itch.

Rosie's feet were freezing in her boots as she stood knocking at the door wondering why she was so weak, why she always did what the others wanted instead of saying, 'Why me? I refuse. It isn't my turn.' The huge farm buildings beyond the house were lit up. Rosie knew what was inside them – poor pathetic hens in cages, hundreds of pigs. Only the sheep still lived natural lives, and for how much longer wondered Rosie, banging the knocker again. She could hear the television on inside, then footsteps coming towards the door. Bolts were undone, a chain released, while Rosie thought, I should have gone to the back; this door is never used. Then Mr Hayward stood before her in felt slippers, cords and enormous sweater, a pipe in one hand.

'Well,' he demanded. 'What brings you here on such a night?'

'I just came to say I am sorry about your sheep being killed, but it wasn't our dog who killed them.' Her teeth were chattering with cold now and, as she spoke, she could see snowflakes falling like shredded paper on to the soft, wet, winter earth.

'You see our Kelly doesn't kill animals, Mr Hayward,' she continued.

'There's always a first time; and he's big and black; that's all I am saying, he's big and black,' and suddenly the words 'big and black' seemed to assume tremendous importance – as though they proved everything, made Kelly guilty, thought Rosie.

'Anyway, he will be on a chain from now onwards,' answered Rosie, while Andy called, 'Ask if we can see the carcases.'

But before Rosie could speak Mr Hayward was shouting, 'No, that you can't. Now you get off home before the snow gets you. I'm keeping my mind open as to what killed three of my best ewes last night. But if I see your black dog up 'ere, he's going to get a bullet straight through his skull; I promise you that.' And with that he slammed the heavy oak door shut.

'You didn't need to shout, Andy,' complained Rosie, mounting Lapwing. 'Everything was going all right until you butted in.'

'You weren't getting anywhere and we need evidence,' replied Andy, looking down at the damp ground. 'Pawmarks, hair on wire, that sort of thing.'

'If the police can't find clues why should we be able to?' asked Rosie.

'The police aren't around all the time, but we are. We've got nothing else to do.'

'And we've got to save Kelly,' said Clara. 'Because Mr Hayward meant what he said and there may be other people who feel the same, hysterical gun-happy people. The sort who shoot at every animal they see and call it "game". Who would boast they had killed the monster when Kelly lay stretched out dead . . .'

'Yes, she's right,' agreed Andy, and all the time the snow was falling faster and now it was no longer melting away but lying, soft wet patches of white in the gathering dusk.

'We can start again tomorrow,' replied Emma, turning homewards, thinking that the Wells children always exaggerated everything, making drama out of nothing.

Their reins were wet and slippery now, their ponies' manes festooned with melting snow. The sky seemed to be growing whiter too and the wind more threatening.

'Yes, first thing, we will get up early,' said Rosie. 'Muck out and feed and be on our way before ten . . .' But even as she said it, she did not really believe it. Because by tomorrow, everything would be a white wilderness. By tomorrow it might be too late to do anything.

But now Andy had drawn rein, was standing in his stirrups shouting, 'Look over there. There's something moving. Look on the ridge by the trees. Look!'

'I can't see anything,' cried Clara.

'I can. Look . . . it's moving.'

'Yes, there is something moving,' confirmed Emma, trying to control the racing of her heart.

'I must get a picture of it . . . I must,' shouted Andy, already galloping towards the ridge.

The ground was ploughed and heavy, dragging at their ponies' legs. Standing in her stirrups, Clara cried, 'So that proves it isn't Kelly.'

24

'But no one will believe us. They'll say we imagined it; that is why I must get a picture of it,' shouted Andy, crouching over Caspar's neck.

'It doesn't look like Kelly. It's not so big for one thing. It looks more like a cat,' cried Rosie.

'Yes. A wild cat,' cried Clara. 'A lynx.'

'Or a black tiger,' shouted Andy laughing.

They reached the ridge and could see pawmarks disappearing beneath the falling snow. 'So it does exist,' said Rosie. 'It wasn't our imagination.'

'Of course it wasn't our imagination,' retorted Andy.

'We'll never find whatever it is now,' said Emma, more sensible than the others. 'I suggest we go home.'

'Not yet. I must get a picture. It can't be far away,' Andy said.

'Well I'm not going a step further. I am going home,' replied Emma, turning Sandpiper round. 'Anyone can see the snow is getting worse and I'm freezing.'

'Don't go. Please don't go yet,' pleaded Rosie.

'I've got my father coming home tonight,' Emma argued over her shoulder, riding away. 'You are all mad, completely mad.'

'And you're scared, plain scared,' shouted Clara, her hands freezing inside her already damp gloves.

'Can't you see, we are doing it for Kelly. Don't you care about Kelly?' shouted Rosie.

'You'll sprain your ponies' tendons and freeze to

death, that's what you will do,' shouted Emma, trotting away, her face numb with cold.

'Don't bother about her,' said Andy, looking at Rosie's anxious face. 'We won't be long, we'll just follow the animal's pawmarks straight to its lair. Don't you see the snow is a godsend.'

'And it will be hours before it's deep,' said Clara.

'Emma has gone home and she's usually right,' replied Rosie.

But Andy was standing in his stirrups again now, shouting, 'Look, I can see it, it's over there . . . it's slinking along the next headland. Come on, gallop.' He had taken his camera off his back and held it now like a pistol ready to shoot. Another second and they were all galloping across newly sown winter wheat — overcome by the excitement of the chase, a thundering in their ears, their hearts thudding against their ribs.

From the bridleway, Emma stopped to look at them — now no more than specks in the distance and soon to disappear completely beyond a line of trees. They are completely mad, she thought again. What on earth shall I tell their parents? Without hope she shouted, 'Come back. It's no good. Come back.' But the wind simply whipped her voice away and lost it in the silence of the falling snow. They'll blame me. What if they blame me? thought Emma, turning homewards again, recalling that the Wells family had come from a town, which meant they had no inbred understanding of the weather, and so could not recognise what the sky had been spelling out so plainly for the last hour. She pushed Sandpiper into a trot and everything seemed empty, every other living thing tucked up somewhere safe except for herself and Sandpiper and her crazy friends.

Mr and Mrs Wells were in the yard when Emma reached Park Farm.

'What's happened? Where are the others?' called Bronwen anxiously as Emma appeared in the drive. David was forking dirty straw on to the midden.

'Why all alone?' he asked putting down his fork.

'They wouldn't come back.'

'What do you mean, wouldn't come back?' David asked, while Bronwen stood behind him, one hand on his shoulder.

'We saw the beast or whatever it's called,' related Emma wearily, running up her stirrups. 'They went in pursuit and wouldn't come back. It's not my fault. I told them they were mad.' She was trying not to feel guilty as Sandpiper pulled her into his loose box and started eating hay while still wearing his bridle. The yard lights were on and the snow was falling faster than ever now, faster than Emma had seen snow fall before.

'I told them to come back,' she repeated, untacking Sandpiper. 'I couldn't make them. They were like hounds after a fox. They were thinking of Kelly. Andy wanted to take a picture of the monster. And I knew Daddy would kill me if I was late home, because I'm supposed to be cooking supper. He's bringing a girl friend home. He's thinking of getting married again. I'm sure I will hate her. But I had to get back, you do see that, don't you? I told them to come home,' she said tearfully.

'It is not your fault,' replied David, carrying her tack to the tack room. 'You go home and get warm. No one is blaming you, love. I'll see to Sandpiper. Run along, love, and if you need any help give us a ring.'

'Are you sure?'

'Quite sure.'

The snow was thick enough for footprints now and it was still falling. David Wells went to the gate and looked down the road. Everything was silent, the road somehow smaller because of the snow. A car slid by, its tyres muffled by the snow; then another and another, all silent like burglars not wishing to be heard, going by with windscreen wipers working silently, their wheels making ridges in the snow . . .

He walked back to the house where he found Bronwen putting the kettle on. 'No sign, not a sign anywhere,' he said, sitting in the basket chair they had brought with them from the town.

'The ponies will bring them home. They'll manage, David,' Bronwen said. 'I will have plenty of warm drinks ready and a good fire burning in the Raeburn.'

'I just wish it would stop snowing,' replied David, pushing a strand of fair hair off his forehead. 'I don't want us cut off. There's so much needs doing.'

Bronwen handed him a mug of tea. Looking out of the window, he realised that the snow made everything look smaller, cosier, closer to you somehow. And it was still falling.

'I just wish they were home,' he said. 'We shouldn't have let them go. It's hard to know sometimes right from wrong – if you're always saying no, you kill their initiative. I did not think they would stay out this long; I just thought they were going to the farm and back.'

'Stop worrying, David, they'll be all right,' said Bronwen, stoking up the Raeburn, putting tea plates on the table, filling the kettle again. 'They'll be frozen, but they'll be all right.'

3

New Year's Eve

'He's gone. We've lost him again,' said Andy, stopping Casper.

They had crossed three fields, scrambled across a ditch, jumped a low stile, their ponies slipping and slithering but filled with the excitement of the chase. Now they were steaming, their long winter coats soaked with melted snow and sweat.

'There's a road over there. We had better push on,' suggested Rosie.

'We could go back,' Clara said.

'But it's getting deeper every minute. And we don't know the way. At least the road will be open and there will be signposts and cars,' Rosie argued.

'But which road is it?' asked Andy. 'And which is the way back?'

They could barely see a metre now, because of the falling snow. The whole landscape was dramatically changed. The fields all looked the same, just an endless sea of white.

'Let's ride towards the telegraph poles over there,' said Andy, pushing Caspar with his legs.

The ponies did not want to go forward. They floundered in the snow which started to ball in their hoofs, so that soon they seemed to be walking on stilts.

'It's hardly four o'clock,' said Rosie, peering at her watch. 'And it won't get dark because of the snow.' It was small consolation. The snow hurt their eyes. The ponies tried persistently to turn their quarters to the wind so that most of the time they were moving sideways. They rode with their heads bent, not knowing when grass turned to plough or winter wheat. Occasionally they floundered over ruts, or stumbled on stones beneath the snow. Lapwing insisted on leading, his head bent.

'We ought to be following the beast's footprints,' Andy said.

'We can't, they are covered with snow,' Rosie answered, hunched and cold. 'Can't you see there's no trace of anything? Nobody will ever find us if we don't keep moving.'

'Shut up,' exclaimed Andy. 'In a moment we will be on a road. We can stop at a house and borrow a shovel.'

'Or telephone home,' suggested Clara.

'I told you we should have listened to Emma,' said Rosie.

'I told you so,' mimicked Andy.

Soon Clara was trying not to cry with cold. Taller

31

and thinner than Rosie, she felt the cold more – her whole face felt numb and her feet seemed to have turned to ice inside her boots and her eyes refused to stop watering so that she couldn't see anything any more, just snow falling faster and faster like a racing engine, or a galloping horse with the wind under his tail. It was impossible to look up at the sky either, anyway she knew without looking that it was promising nothing but more snow.

Rosie had pulled her collar round her ears but it no longer kept the snow out, so that she was soaked underneath.

Andy was thinking of home, of Mum and Dad looking out of the windows, anxiously waiting, listening for muffled hoof beats, hearing nothing. Soon, he thought, they will start a search. Emma will help, will say, 'They went that way.' But they won't be able to see anything, not a metre in front of them – and that to Andy seemed the most terrifying thing of all. It's like being blind, he thought; or wrapped in a blanket of whiteness. And it's not going to stop and we are going to be buried in it. The ponies were losing heart and now only wanted to stand with their tails to the wind waiting for the snow to stop, and the wind was growing faster every moment until it was sweeping across the open fields like a howling gale, driving the snow into drifts, burying hedges and fences alike.

I'm not going to cry, thought Rosie. We won't be buried. This is sane, beautiful England. Someone will find us. Soon we will be home in front of the Raeburn with hot mugs of tea in our hands, the ponies safe in their loose boxes. Then this will seem like nothing but a bad dream.

'We must reach the road, don't give up,' shouted Andy. 'It's only a few metres away.'

But the others failed to hear him for the wind whisked his voice away as it left his lips.

Emma was telephoning. 'Is that Bronwen? Are they back yet?' she asked, her voice shaking.

'No, not a sign. David is just setting out to look, while I man the telephone,' Bronwen answered, her voice high with anxiety.

'I feel like a deserter. Can I do anything to help?' asked Emma.

'You're not a deserter. You are the only one with any sense. I wish they had listened to you. I do really,' said Bronwen, sobbing.

'I'm sorry.' Emma put down the telephone. Bronwen's tears unnerved her. She wished her father would come home, for he always had an answer to problems. He would know what to do. In the meantime she peeled potatoes, chopped onions, washed cauliflower mechanically, for a prospective stepmother she did not want, who was only twenty five and already divorced.

David Wells was on the telephone now, borrowing a landrover. No one seemed very helpful or optimistic. 'You won't get far even in a landrover,' they said. And it was still snowing. He put down the receiver. 'Okay, a thermos of coffee, blankets, what else do I need, love?' he asked Bronwen.

'A shovel, boots, warm sweaters,' cried Bronwen, dashing upstairs.

Evening had come without them noticing. Normally at this time all the animals would be settled for the night. It was one of the best times, when they all sat down together at the plain wood table with steaming mugs in their hands. Just a few minutes between work and the telly taking over, a time for talking. Now the house without the children seemed empty and uninhabited; the table laid in the kitchen was waiting for children who might never return. Bronwen could not put such feelings into words. Looking at her face David said, 'Don't worry, love, they will have found shelter somewhere.'

'But where's the landrover? Time is passing. Every minute and the snow gets deeper,' cried Bronwen.

'Give Reg time. He may not make it.'

'May not make it? What do you mean?'

'He's got to dig his way out. He's fifty metres from the road. He lives at Crabtree farm; it's nearly two kilometres away.'

'But the road is still open.'

'I hope so,' said David.

*

The children had reached the road at last. The snow lay in drifts packed against hedges, but once the hedges ended there was no difference between roads and fields. There were still a few cars running, their tyres skidding, sending up a smell of burning rubber; their engines revving up, struggling, stopping, starting; their exhausts filling the air with carbon dioxide. Rosie waved her arms and shouted. A man leaned out of the window to call, 'Sorry, I daren't stop.' His windscreen wipers were clogged with snow. Then for a moment, sheltered by hedges, they could see one another.

'I think we are going to perish,' cried Clara, looking at Rosie.

'No, we will be rescued. In a minute we'll see a snow plough, then the Council's gritting lorries. We'll be all right now,' shouted Andy.

'The police will rescue us. They'll have the road cleared and send a horsebox for the ponies,' shouted Rosie.

'I think my feet are frozen. I think I'm suffering from frostbite and that means they'll be cut off, doesn't it?' shouted Clara.

'No, not nowadays,' said Andy, but he was no longer sure, no longer sure of anything.

And then suddenly there were no more cars, just themselves and the falling snow and, except for the wind, an awful silence pressing down on them, smothering them as much as the snow falling.

'We had better move on,' said Andy.

35

'It will be worse further on,' argued Rosie.

'But there may be houses further on, help, hot drinks, warm clothes, a telephone,' said Andy.

'I want a doctor, my feet are dying. I can feel them dying,' cried Clara.

'Don't be silly, this isn't the Arctic,' shouted Rosie. The ponies did not wish to move. 'They may be right, they may know more than us,' suggested Rosie.

'But not about telephones and civilisation,' argued Andy. 'I wish I recognised this road . . .'

'It doesn't matter, because we are not going to reach home, are we?' asked Clara. 'We can only hope that someone will take pity on us.'

'It's better with hedges. Out there it's like a desert,' cried Rosie.

'But the desert can't last for ever,' shouted Andy.

'I wish we had listened to Emma,' cried Rosie. 'Why didn't we?'

'Because of the beast,' Andy reminded her. 'What's the time?'

Rosie looked at her watch. 'Six o'clock,' she yelled.

'It can't be.'

'Well it is.'

They pushed their ponies on, Lapwing leading again, ploughing through knee-deep snow, stopping to rest every few minutes. Then they were outside the shelter of the hedges and the wind hit them like a hurricane, whipping their faces with snow, turning everything into a whirling world of white.

'Let's go back,' yelled Clara.

'Yes,' shouted Rosie.

But now the ponies would not turn back, and seemed resigned to struggling on, while each moment the snow grew deeper and the wind seemed fiercer until speech was impossible, and they were each lost in a shuttered space of whirling snow, oblivious of anything but the wish to stay alive. Rosie thought of Emma cooking a meal, looking out of the window from time to time at the falling snow. How wise she had been! How sensible! How easy it was to make a mistake and die for it, decided Rosie – and didn't want to die.

Clara thought about her feet being cut off, of waking up without them in some unknown hospital; while Andy imagined his parents setting out to look for them. They will never find us, that's obvious, for cars cannot move in such a world; only a helicopter can help us now, he thought.

They hardly knew now whether they were on road or field, only the telegraph posts guided them, their wires sagging, weighted down by snow. They were still riding, but hardly moving any more. Casper appeared exhausted; in places the snow reached to his chest; twice he nearly fell; and the raging snowstorm drove them sideways so that several times they found themselves in drifts and it was an immense struggle to get out again. And the fear in their hearts instead of spurring them on had a deadening effect, so that it was easy to think, let's stop and rest; there's no point in going on any more. Yet they knew too that to stop was to be buried.

Then, at last, they saw houses far away, half buried in snow; small and dreamlike in the distance, looking like houses made of icing sugar. Rosie stared, then shouted despairingly, 'We'll never make it, will we?'

Clara thought, I'm dreaming; those aren't houses, they are there because I want them to be there. And now none of them could look up for more than a few seconds so blinding was the snow. It was then they saw the beast staring down at them from a buried bank, so covered with snow that only his eyes showed, filled with greed. Clara screamed and the ponies raised their heads in terror. 'He's going to eat us,' screamed Rosie.

'Us or the ponies,' shouted Andy.

Emma picked up the telephone receiver which was pale ivory and in the kitchen. 'Yes, what is it?' she asked, one eye on the curry cooking on the stove.

'We can't make it. We are in a hotel fifty kilometres away. We can't get through,' her father said.

'What do you mean – can't get through? I've cooked dinner. It's all ready, even the table is set. I left the Wells children in the snow, deserted them to return here to cook dinner for you,' Emma shouted, furious at hours of wasted cooking.

'What do you mean "left the Wells children in the snow"?'

'We were looking for the beast, you know the one in the newspapers. They saw him; they wouldn't come back . . .' Emma was near to tears now.

There was a short silence before her father asked, 'Didn't they hear the warnings on television and radio?' And Emma could hear voices in the background as she said, 'No. You know they hardly ever listen to the radio and television is out of bounds in their house until five o'clock.'

'Is someone looking for them?'

'I don't know. I have been waiting here cooking your beastly dinner.'

'What a mess! I will ring up later. Don't worry, darling. Will you be all right all alone?'

'I shall have to be, won't I? I just wish I had a dog,' said Emma, replacing the receiver slowly. She switched off the heat beneath the curry, then went to the window to look out, feeling sick inside, wishing that she had a brother or sister, someone else to share her anxiety.

And it is New Year's Eve, she remembered.

'Here comes the landrover,' said David, picking up thermos, blankets and a torch, while Bronwen followed with a shovel.

Another minute and Reg was standing in the doorway. 'We won't get far, they say the turnpike's cut off.' He wore a cap, old sheepskin coat, thick trousers, boots, no gloves. He had lived in the area all his life and still called the main road, 'the turnpike'. 'I've brought my double bore with me, just in case we see the beast,' he said, taking the shovel from Bronwen. 'And a couple of terriers game for anything.' He had a country smell about him, a mixture of cow, silage and tobacco, thought Bronwen.

'You must find them. Just lock the ponies up somewhere and bring our kids home safe and sound,' she said.

She wished she could go with them, for anything would be better than waiting, and hoping, watching the minutes turn into hours.

The landrover skidded as it turned. David had dug out a track as far as the gate. It was still snowing; the windscreen wipers on the landrover were already clogged with it and unable to move, the tyres were clogged thick with it and the sky had not changed but was the same cruel grey it had been for hours.

Bronwen had no illusions as she returned indoors. She knew that the landrover would not be able to travel very far. It was just one effort that had to be made, to prove that they had tried. She would ring the police, the hospitals, the county council. It was six o'clock now so most likely the county council offices would be shut, but she would still try. Kelly thumped his tail at her, grovelled at her feet, asking for forgiveness when there was nothing to forgive.

She dialled the local police station. 'My children are out in the snow on three ponies. Can you help?' she asked, without hope in her voice.

The voice at the other end called her madam; told her that all the cars had been called in, that they wouldn't be sent out again that night.

'Surely you heeded the warnings given on radio and television,' the voice asked.

'We didn't hear them . . .' Bronwen said.

'We can't do anything, love,' the voice at the other end was suddenly warmer. 'Someone will have taken them in. Don't worry, love.'

'Shall I try the hospitals?' she asked next.

'The ambulances can't get out.'

She put down the receiver while he was still talking. Her world seemed to be falling apart. How could the police refuse to help? It was inconceivable.

She made a pot of tea mechanically, drank a mug of it without noticing. She almost went outside to fill up haynets for the ponies, then remembered that she had remained to man the telephone. She switched on the television, but the picture was blurred and the news over, so she switched it off again.

Then Emma rang. 'Daddy's snowed up some-where. Are they back?' she asked, her voice high with anxiety.

'No, not a sign. David's gone out in a landrover to look.'

'You will ring me when they get back, won't you?'

'Yes of course.'

'Is Kelly still with you?'

'Yes. Do you want to come over?'

'No, I don't think so. Daddy's going to ring again. I think I had better be here. You've tried the police?'

'Yes, they've called in all their cars . . .' Bronwen's voice relayed her despair. 'It's the waiting I hate. The not being able to do anything,' she said.

'Same here,' agreed Emma.

And the snow was still falling, that was the worst thing of all, thought Emma drawing the curtains, knowing that she would not be able to sleep until Andy, Rosie and Clara were home again. Damn the beast, damn everything, she thought, turning on the television.

4

Take it easy

The beast had gone as quickly as he had appeared.

'Listen,' shouted Andy. 'Listen. Can you hear a tractor?' Their hands had lost all feeling inside their gloves. They had dismounted and were battling through the snow dragging their ponies after them.

The tractor came nearer. The driver shouted, 'Follow me,' gesticulating wildly, and drove on leaving ruts in the snow along which they struggled, passing lines of stranded cars, pulling their exhausted mounts after them.

'Why don't their occupants get out,' shouted Rosie. 'This could be their last chance.'

Some of the cars had their engines on. A woman stood in the blizzard in overcoat, tights or stockings and high heels. 'Fetch help,' she cried. 'I can't walk anywhere as I am. I shall die up here.'

Rosie tried to answer but it was useless against the raging blizzard, and her words died before they reached the freezing air.

Andy had tried to photograph the beast, but his

hands were so numb he had dropped his camera on to the shifting snow and the wind had swept it away.

The houses grew closer. Lights cast pools of yellow light on the whiteness of the snow. Chimneys sent thin smoke into the cold, grey air. Cars stood abandoned along the street . . .

The houses sheltered them, breaking the force of the blizzard so that they were able to raise their heads and look about them again. The tractor driver had stopped, was standing in the street. 'Put your ponies in the yard here,' he said, opening a gate. 'It's not much of a place, but it will have to do.'

'We saw the beast,' Clara cried.

'Never mind the beast, do as I say.'

There were open buildings round a brick yard, no straw nor hay, no sign of water.

'But—' began Rosie.

'No buts. Do as you're told.'

They took off their tack with numb fingers.

'Leave it in the shed, that's right, under cover. You had best come along to The Greyhound; get in the dry,' the man said. He was wearing boots, an ancient mackintosh tied round his waist with binder twine, a cap which only covered part of his grey hair. 'You shouldn't be out in weather like this,' he said disapprovingly, shutting the yard gate after them.

'What about hay?' asked Rosie anxiously.

'They'll survive.'

The Greyhound was full of people. The landlord scowled at them. 'What are you doing out in this weather?'

'We were chasing the beast, the monster,' Andy answered, wishing he had money in his pocket.

Rosie was thinking the same thing.

'What, tonight?' someone exclaimed. 'You must need your heads examined. Didn't you hear the warnings?'

'No.' Clara felt near to tears. Rosie was still worrying about the ponies. They could hear the tractor starting up again outside.

'What about the cars on the hill? Aren't you going to rescue the people up there? Shall I ring the police?' Rosie asked.

'The police are not helping anyone tonight,' the landlord said, while his wife pulled tankards of beer for a bunch of men sitting near a coal fire.

'You can't stay here anyway,' she said. 'You are under age, and we're full up.'

'Where can we go then?' asked Clara.

'That's your problem, isn't it? You should have known better than to set out on a night like this. What were your parents thinking of?' She had bleached hair, a tight short dress which showed off her boney knees.

'We only meant to be out for half an hour,' Rosie explained.

'We got lost,' added Andy.

'We can't help that, you are under age,' she repeated.

'I'll telephone home,' Rosie said.

'We've no money,' answered Andy, looking like a whipped dog.

'I can reverse the charges,' Rosie replied.

'The lines are down,' said the landlady, sounding pleased.

The bar had a streamer above it proclaiming 'A Happy New Year'.

'That's that then. We're stuck, can't go any further,' said Reg, jumping from the landrover, while his terriers yapped wildly in the back. 'We'll have to dig her out. Give me a shovel, will you, David?'

'But we've only covered five kilometres . . .'

'I can't help that. You can see how deep the snow is and it's getting worse all the time. Come on, give us a hand or we will be here till Domesday.'

'What are we going to do?' cried David, holding his head in his hands.

'Nothin', we can't do nothin', hop in will you, turn her on, not too much choke, second gear, gently does it.'

'We can't just leave them to perish,' said David, turning the ignition on.

'They won't perish. Someone will take them in.'

'What, ponies and all?'

'We'll have to hope so, give her a bit more choke.

No, she won't move. There's some sacks in the back, try them under the tyres. Come on, get moving, David. We don't want to be here all night.'

'I'm doing my best. I'm not used to these conditions. I'm more used to the desert and that can be just as deadly,' said David.

Bronwen had taken the kettle off and was sitting with her head in her hands. She blamed herself. I should have stopped the children riding out, have said, 'No, not tonight,' she thought. But she hadn't and there was no changing that undeniable fact, and now the children could die and it would be her fault entirely. She could see it all — the inevitable headlines, CHILDREN PERISH IN BLIZZARD. Reporters would visit the farm when the snow was gone with a mass of heart-rending questions. Television would show pictures of them.

Kelly was lying in a corner. He was abject, seemingly convinced that he had caused a tragedy. And in a way he had, thought Bronwen, because if he had not been here, he would not have been accused, and the children would not have disappeared in pursuit of the monster . . . But it was too late now to do anything. She could only sit and wait.

Emma was going to bed. She did not want to think about the Wells children any more. She wanted to wake in the morning and discover that everything was all right, that they were back at home, as mad as ever, with their ponies peacefully munching hay. But she knew it could not be like that, because no one could get home on such a night – which meant that they were either holed up somewhere warm and safe, or actually dying, or dead already. And now she hated snow and knew she would never look at it again without loathing. If only it was just a bad dream, she thought. If only Daddy was here to say, 'Don't worry, everything is going to be all right.'

If only I wasn't alone.

'You can't leave those people in their cars,' said Rosie. 'They will die.' And at last people started to stir, to talk about getting out tractors and trailers. The bunch of men by the fire turned up their coat collars and went out into the night while an older man bought the children bags of crisps. 'You won't get home tonight,' he said, as though they did not know.

'They can't stay,' the landlord said.

They could hear tractors starting up now, men's voices. The wind had dropped and when Rosie looked out everything was still and white, the inn sign gently creaking, a cat stealing over the snow, a Christmas Card scene with a moon rising above it all. 'I wish we could telephone home,' she said. 'Mum and Dad must be so worried.'

'I wish I had money. I'm so hungry,' said Andy.

'I wish we had somewhere to sleep. But there's no room at the Inn,' Clara said.

It was nine o'clock now; then ten o'clock. The children leaned against a radiator, their clothes steaming. Rosie was worrying about the ponies again. Andy about their parents. Clara was wishing she had stayed at home and was now tucked up in bed, with the curtains drawn back so that she could see the snow sparkling in the moonlight.

Presently they heard the tractors returning, the sound of voices. Then a man leaning against the bar, red cheeked, dark haired, about thirty five, said, 'You can stay with me if you like. But you'll have to sleep on the floor. My place is called the Old Stable.'

Clara smiled then, thinking if only it were Christmas night! They picked up their hats and followed the man out into a starlit night which made the village look like a stage set. The snow was crisp under their feet. They ran ahead to look at the ponies. Someone had given them hay and buckets of water; all the same they raised their heads and whinnied.

'I wish we could telephone home,' repeated Rosie.

The Old Stable was down a lane near the church. It did not resemble a stable any more, but was painted white with metal windows and a door bell which went ding dong. 'Call me Paul,' the man said,

49

making them toast, spreading butter on it. 'There's
nothing else to eat, because the wife's in hospital.'

He put mattresses on the floor in front of an
open fire which he made up with logs and huge
lumps of coal. And now they were warm for the
first time in hours. He made them steaming mugs
of tea and fetched them towels and pointed out
the bathroom.

'All right? Anything else you want?' he asked.

They had taken off their boots, left them in the
porch. Their gloves were lying in front of the fire
now drying.

'It's lovely. I just wish we could telephone our
parents,' Rosie said yet again.

'We'll try,' Paul said. 'What's the number?'

But the lines were still down and that seemed the
worst thing of all.

They took their coats off, lay in front of the fire
talking. They were tired but could not sleep; then
one by one they dropped off.

David was back now, drinking tea in the kitchen
with Bronwen. 'They'll be all right,' he said for the
third time.

'I don't know how.'

'They're not fools.'

'They are only kids. If they don't come back . . .'

'Don't be ridiculous,' David said.

'It's not ridiculous. Emma's father hasn't got
home. She's all alone; it isn't right.'

'Emma's not a kid any more, and we'll be able to laugh about it next week,' said David.

'Listen, there's a wild animal howling,' cried Bronwen.

'You're imagining it. You're tired out. Come to bed.'

'I'm going to stay up. They may telephone. The wires may be up again soon,' Bronwen said.

'You're quite mad. No one can get to the wires. We are all cut off.'

Dawn came at last, a terrible freezing dawn with everything completely still, nothing moving, the trees sagging beneath their burden of snow.

David fell asleep then, slumped in a chair, while Bronwen stood at the window looking out and snow started to fall again, gently this time like white confetti. For once there was no sound of cars moving through the village, no milkman rattling bottles, no red post van. It was as though everything had ground to a halt, had run down as a clock runs down. They are alive or dead, thought Bronwen, wearily making up the Raeburn.

Kelly was lying at David's feet.

'Great slob, useless creature. I wish you had never come here. I wish you were dead. You've caused everything to go wrong. You're an ill omen,' Bronwen told him, her voice heavy with dislike. But, misunderstanding her, he stood up wagging his tail and waiting hopefully for breakfast, his eyes gleaming.

'You can wait, and if they die I will never forgive you,' Bronwen said, before going outside. David had cleared a way to the yard the evening before, but the snow still reached to her knees and because she was imagining her children buried and dying, it was some time before she noticed the heap of skin and bones lying in the snow. She stared; then started to shiver uncontrollably. It's Tansy, she thought, running towards the house. Tansy, the best kid we've ever had.

Throwing her weight against the back door she almost fell into the kitchen, shouting, 'Tansy's dead. Wake up, David. The monster's been and he's killed Tansy.'

Tansy had been stabled in one of the old pigsties. The wall was low around the open part. Obviously the monster or beast had killed her silently, then lifted her over the wall before eating her in the snow. It was too horrible to contemplate yet it had happened, thought Bronwen, shaking David awake.

They went out into the snow together and stood arms interlocked while Bronwen's tears froze on her cheeks.

'It's more cunning than a fox. We ought to tell the police . . .' said David.

'But we can't, can we?' asked Bronwen.

'I could walk to the police station.'

'You are not leaving here again, not until the children are home safe and sound,' replied Bronwen, thinking, *if* they are still alive.

'Take it easy. Keep calm. Let's have a nice cup of tea and talk things over, love,' David said. 'The monster or beast, whatever you call him, must be very quiet, otherwise Kelly would have heard him,' he continued. 'He must have struck quite early before I was back.'

'I heard him. You said I was imagining it or words to that effect. Don't you remember?' asked Bronwen angrily. 'And as for Kelly, he's useless. He's a lap dog.' She finished pouring hot water on to the tea leaves. 'Anyway Tansy does not matter, not compared to Clara, Andy and Rosie, nothing matters compared to that.' She handed David a mug of tea. 'If they die, I don't want to go on living; it's as simple as that.'

'Someone will have taken them in. The main problem now is that the monster has tasted blood in our yard, so he will be back. And we know it was not Kelly, because he was with you all night. I shall have to make all the doors secure, shut them top and bottom; and move the goats elsewhere,' David said, pulling on his boots. 'And it's seven o'clock, Bronwen – milking time.'

'I don't know how we can go on living normally; it's grotesque,' complained Bronwen.

'Even in wars, cows must be milked,' insisted David. 'And today is the beginning of a New Year.'

'And a fine celebration we've had,' said Bronwen.

5

Blood on the snow

'We had better see the ponies,' cried Rosie. She had woken first, knowing instantly where she was, while Clara, stretching like a cat, asked, 'Where am I? What's happened?', and Andy, who had finally slept in a chair, sat rubbing his eyes trying to remember the night before.

'We *must* see to the ponies,' cried Rosie, looking for her boots. She drew back the curtains. The sun was shining and everything outside was indescribably beautiful. Ten minutes later they were in the street, then running to the yard which held their ponies. 'They must be starving,' Rosie said.

Nothing was moving. Only the church clock told them it was eight o'clock. The ponies whinnied, and nudged the children looking for food. Their water buckets were upset, the hay of the night before gone. Rosie found a tap, but though she turned it on, no water ran.

'We'll come back later,' Andy said.

'After we've telephoned home,' Rosie said.

They found a kiosk, dialled their number, but the line was still dead. 'We must be able to get news to them somehow,' cried Clara. The sun shone brighter, and people started to emerge from their houses dressed for snow. Then everyone seemed to be tramping up the hill to look at the stranded cars, to peer through their windows looking for people inside. More people emerged carrying shovels.

'Where's the snow plough?' asked a tall man with straw-coloured hair.

'The diesel oil has frozen,' said a man dressed for skiing.

'Typical,' said someone else.

And the children went with them like flotsam carried by a tide. They peered through windows too and it was impossible to believe that only hours ago a blizzard had raged turning the road into a living hell.

'We had better go back to Paul,' said Rosie in sudden panic. So they ran down the hill on the now crisp snow.

There was a smell of burnt toast inside The Old Stable. 'They are working on the telephone. Sit down, it's breakfast time now.' They could see Paul better now that they were no longer exhausted; he had a square flabby face, dark hair, strong shoulders, short legs.

'I hope it clears. I want to see my wife in hospital. She may have had the baby for all I know,' he said.

'How do you know they are mending the telephone?' asked Rosie.

'Because there's a funny noise going on inside the receiver,' he said.

They ate the toast with marmalade; there was nothing else. And now they could see a snow plough going past the windows.

'We had better tack up,' cried Rosie.

'Take it easy. It will take them hours to clear even ten kilometres of road and you don't want to get stranded again, do you?' asked Paul.

'But the ponies are starving.'

'They will survive.'

Soon he took them up the hill in his van. Men were digging out the cars and getting them going again, while people stood in groups watching. The air smelt of exhaust fumes. They went back to the Old Stable and tried the telephone again.

'It's ringing,' cried Andy, clutching the receiver.

Bronwen answered. 'It's Andy, we're all right,' Andy cried while Rosie and Clara leaned over him breathing down his neck.

'Where are you? Are you hurt?' Bronwen was in the kitchen with the radio on.

'We're in a village called Langsdowne and we're all right.'

'What about the ponies?'

'They are all right too.'

'We will come and fetch you.'

'The road isn't open yet.'

'We'll bring spades and shovels then; and boots and coffee,' cried Bronwen, laughing.

'Are you all right?' shrieked Rosie, seizing the receiver.

'Yes and no.'

'We'll be by the church. But we'll be riding home,' cried Andy, wrenching the receiver away from Rosie.

'We'll see you then, by the church. We may take a bit of time getting through because they haven't cleared our road yet,' said Bronwen.

'They are working like mad here,' Andy said before putting down the receiver.

They went outside again, took toast crusts to the ponies. A woman in a nearby house opened a door to call, 'Do you want water for your horses? Come into my kitchen and help yourselves.' She moved cups off a draining board and they filled two buckets with water. But the ponies didn't drink.

'They must have been licking the snow,' Andy said.

They fetched their things from the Old Stable, thanked Paul, stood by the church. The sky was a bright blue now, but the snow wasn't melting. People were sweeping it from their doorsteps while children threw snowballs at one another. A car passed through, very slowly, covered in snow, then another and another. And further away a snow plough was heaping snow along the roadside, making a narrow lane so the cars could squeeze through.

They went back to their ponies then. 'Let's tack up,' suggested Clara. The tack was sodden, the leather like cardboard.

It was eleven o'clock when they returned to the church. 'They are taking a long time,' complained Clara, who hated waiting.

'Our road has to be cleared,' said Rosie. 'Oh I do so want to get home. I feel as though we've been away for days instead of just one night.'

'And I'm starving,' said Andy. 'Look, my jodhpurs won't stay up any more.'

'Me too. My whole inside is aching with hunger,' complained Clara.

Cars were moving both ways now, slowly, uncertainly, like people feeling their way in the dark. And there was a constant sound of machines in action, for there were farmers now working with fork lifts as well as the county council men with snow ploughs.

The church clock struck twelve, while a smell of cooking drifted out from The Greyhound making Andy's mouth water.

'I wish they would hurry,' Rosie said.

'Perhaps Emma will come with them,' suggested Clara.

'If we had set off an hour ago, we would be home by now. It can't be more than ten kilometres,' said Andy.

'If we had any money we could buy crisps at the pub,' said Clara.

Then they saw a cattle truck coming slowly through the village. It stopped near the church. 'Oh there you are,' shouted David.

'We didn't expect you in a cattle truck,' shouted Andy. 'We were going to ride home.'

'I borrowed it. Are you all right? Where are the ponies?' cried Dad, leaping down.

'We'll get them. Is everything all right at home?' asked Rosie.

'More or less.'

'Something's died, hasn't it? What is it? Which animal? Come on Dad, own up. You can't hide it from us,' said Clara, standing directly in Dad's path, upright and accusing.

'I'll tell you on the way home.'

Dad had brought headcollars and ropes; the ponies loaded easily, Lapwing going first. 'Where's Mum?' Rosie wanted to know, tying him up.

'Cooking lunch.'

So she is all right, thought Rosie.

'Were you worried?' Clara asked, as they turned the screws on the ramp.

'Your mother was. We tried to get to you, but it was too deep,' Dad said, starting the engine. 'I borrowed a landrover. Reg Palmer came with me, but we hardly got any way at all. Where did you spend the night?'

They started to relate their experiences. 'We saw

the monster. I took a picture of him, but lost the camera,' said Andy. He realized now that it was impossible to explain the utter terror of the blizzard, for it was fading already from his mind; time blurring the edges of the terror he had felt.

'We thought we were going to die,' Rosie told him and he touched her hand, saying, 'We thought so too. What a night! I never want to live through the like of it again. We'll have to reward the chap who put you up. Was his place really called the Old Stable?'

'Yes, that's right,' Clara said.

They could see their own village now, looking smaller in the snow.

'The ponies were marvellous,' Rosie said.

Bronwen was waiting for them at the gate, calling, 'There's hot water bottles in all your beds. Dad will see to the ponies.'

'But we are all right, Mum. We're not even frost-bitten,' Rosie called, thinking that her mother looked exhausted. 'We are quite all right, honestly, Mum.'

'Emma's been marvellous. She helped this morning. I couldn't have managed without her,' Mum said. 'But now her father is back with her prospective stepmother and she's having to stay home, poor kid.'

They unboxed the ponies, gave them water and hay, took off their boots in the porch, sat down to a lunch of mince and mashed potatoes, followed by apple pie.

'Tell us everything,' Mum said.

The three children took it in turns to speak. When they had finished, Rosie said, 'Now let's have your side of the story.'

Then Mum told them about the long night, about Emma being alone and Dad setting out in a strange landrover and not returning for three hours. 'I've had enough anxiety for a lifetime,' she finished.

'You've missed out something,' Clara said.

'What would that be?'

'Something was killed, wasn't it? I saw blood on the snow,' Clara said.

'Yes. It was Tansy.'

'By the beast?' asked Andy, after a short horrified silence.

'We think so.'

'He'll strike again, won't he? He'll keep striking,' cried Clara dramatically.

'Not if we kill him,' Dad said. 'I've got my double-barrelled shotgun loaded ready. Don't touch it. Do you hear? Don't touch it.'

'And there's Kelly,' said Rosie, getting down on her knees to stroke him.

'He wouldn't hurt a fly,' Mum answered.

'We must find weapons. Have you told the police?' asked Andy.

'Not yet, we were too busy finding you.'

'It's serious, isn't it? I mean we've got so many animals, haven't we?' asked Andy anxiously. 'And they're valuable.'

61

'I've moved the goats,' said Dad.

'Poor Tansy,' cried Clara suddenly, bursting into tears. 'She was so young and sweet. It's so sad.'

'Keep a sense of proportion. You might have died,' Dad said.

'He'll come again. He'll keep coming now. I know he will,' cried Clara.

'We'll make booby traps for him. Keep watch all night,' said Andy.

'Like on a ship,' said Rosie.

It was past two o'clock now. They had eaten lunch without noticing what they ate. Dad rang the police station. Rosie changed into jeans and a polo-necked sweater. Andy found a bell. It had been in the kitchen when they arrived and was like an old-fashioned school bell. 'We can ring this all night,' he said, 'on the hour and the half hour.'

'It's snowing again,' said Clara.

'We had better settle the animals. Come on,' said Bronwen, pulling on boots.

'The police are not interested. They are still getting people out of drifts and there's been a break-in at Hanger Hall,' Dad told them, and they saw how tired he was, so tired that he could hardly stand.

'Go to bed, Dad, we can manage,' Clara said.

Mum didn't look much better. 'Go to bed too. We'll wake you at four with a cup of tea,' Rosie added.

'Are you sure you can manage?'

'Of course we can. We're not five years old,' Clara answered.

'I hope we don't get cut off again,' said Mum, taking off her boots. 'I will do the milking; be sure and wake us . . .'

In the yard everything was turmoil. The goats needed cleaning out and the ponies needed grooming; the hens and bantams, and fancy ducks and wild geese needed feeding too. They all seemed to be asking for food at once, whinnying, mooing, grunting or simply following the children around, pecking at their shoes. Every time they went to the feedhouse they were followed by a crowd of animals all jostling to be first. Only the peacocks stood aloof, waiting miserably in their pen.

There were lists in the feedhouse telling what each animal needed, and scales, nets, dishes and buckets. The water tap had to be thawed out with a kettle of hot water from the house and there was a small grey mouse in the oat bin, which made Clara scream. In the middle of it all Emma appeared to feed Sandpiper.

'Hullo stranger,' Rosie said.

'You got back then, lunatics,' retorted Emma, looking sane and well organised as she always did, without a hair out of place, her finger-nails varnished.

'Is your father back?' asked Andy, stuffing hay into nets.

'Yes.'

'With your prospective stepmother?'

'Yes.'

'Do you like her?'

'I don't know. She's only six years older than I am,' Emma said.

The snow was falling faster now. The wheels of the wheelbarrows were clogged with it and it blew into their faces making their eyes water. The sheep were penned up in a barn. The goats were there too, in a pen fenced with old-fashioned hurdles.

'We must remember to bolt the doors,' Andy said.

Emma knew about Tansy. She had heard the beast howling in the night, she told them. 'It sent a shiver down my spine I can tell you,' she added.

'We had better lock all the doors, top and bottom,' Rosie said. 'Shall I take the first shift?'

'We can arrange that later,' Andy answered.

Suddenly they were all on edge; they had not combed their hair since the day before and Rosie's face was smudged with a mixture of dirt and tears.

Emma changed Sandpiper's rugs, removed muck with a skip, weighed his feed, cutting his oats because he had not been exercised all day. She was very methodical whereas Rosie, Clara and Andy kept bumping into one another and always needed the same tool at the same moment, and two of them fed the small black pigs which were part of the Pet's Corner, so that they ended up having double rations.

Comedian the vanner, who used to work in the walled garden, needed his hoofs picked out. Large the shire horse had squashed his plastic bucket into a flat pancake. Then Little the black Shetland pony knocked Rosie over and, galloping out of his box, made for the fields.

'He should be out anyway,' said Emma laughing. 'Honestly, Shetlands don't need to come in even in snow.'

'He must, because of the beast,' said Andy, fetching oats in a bucket. But Little refused to be caught. He galloped from field to field, lay down and rolled in the snow, paced like a mustang, his tiny head high, his tail over his back, his snorts sounding like a foghorn on a wet night.

'Let him calm down,' advised Emma. 'Don't give him anything to eat.' Emma always seemed to know the answers. She was like her father who was forever telling Mr Wells to take up factory and arable farming. 'Think of all the subsidies you could apply for,' he would say. 'Money for cutting down the hedges, more money for digging out ditches . . .'

As if the Wells did not love their hedges, which were full of birds' nests in spring and summer, and were windbreaks in the winter.

'And then you could let your hedges grow up a bit and then cut them all down again; it's simple,' said Emma's father. 'Money for jam.'

'We are not interested,' Dad had said.

'You'll never grow rich.'

'We don't want to grow rich,' which wasn't true, of course, but Dad said it to stop Emma's father going on and on about money, a subject he never left alone for long.

Now Little was standing with his back to one of the hedges waiting to be pursued. 'Don't go near him. Leave him alone,' said Emma again. 'He's just playing games!'

Dusk had come, a cold grey winter dusk, when Rosie ran indoors to wake her parents. The day was nearly over now. Soon they would all go inside and grow warm and sleepy. There was just Little still to be caught and Marigold to be milked and the doors to be checked on all the buildings, and then a long night, thought Rosie, looking out into the snow, praying that the beast would not come again.

6

No vet

'He won't be caught and that's that,' Dad said, standing in the moonlight holding a halter behind his back. 'He wants to stay out.'

'But the beast will kill him,' cried Clara, staring at a defiant Little. 'We can't leave him out. I shan't sleep a wink.'

'Well I am not staying out here all night,' Dad said.

They had tried everything, coaxing the small black Shetland, tempting him with oats, with sugar beet, with carrots. They had tried driving him gently into the yard. Emma had given up long ago and was now sitting drinking coffee at home. Mum had taken the milk from Marigold into the house and had strained it before pouring it into jugs, and was now laying the table for supper. The snow had stopped falling nearly an hour ago and was crisp and sparkling.

'I will go on trying,' said Rosie. 'He may be better with just me.' So the others returned indoors, while she stood talking to Little. 'It's all right, little pony,' she said. 'There's a feed waiting for you; why don't you follow me into your box?' She held out a bucket of feed, but he merely looked the other way, refusing to be tempted. And slowly Rosie's feet grew numb in her Wellington boots, and her hands turned to ice in her thin woollen gloves.

'Oh don't come in then,' she shouted, losing her temper. 'Stay out and be killed; it will be your funeral.' She threw the bucket down, then went indoors and found the others sitting down to supper.

'Well?' asked Clara.

'No luck.'

'Who is taking the first shift?' Andy asked. 'They can sit in my room if they like. There's a moon so we can see the monster.'

'I will,' offered Rosie, 'because I'm so tired I can't possibly get up at midnight. It will kill me. But what about Little?'

'He will have to stay where he is,' Dad said.

Later Rosie sat outside Andy's room at the top of the old back stairs. She sat on a stiff upright chair staring through a small lattice window at the sleeping snow-covered buildings and beyond to the walled garden, and then to the rooftops of the new neo-Georgian houses where Emma lived. It was very quiet outside in the moonlight and so beautiful that it brought a lump to Rosie's throat. She was so tired that three times she nodded off to wake with a jerk and a feeling of panic, but always the scene was just the same, reminding her of Christmas cards. At one thirty she crept downstairs to Clara's room which was strewn with clothes and smelt like a hairdresser's salon. Clara was asleep with one long-fingered hand stretched across her duvet which was patterned with tiny flowers.

'Wake up. It's your turn.' Rosie touched her hand.

'Go away, I'm sleeping,' Clara said.

'It's your watch. Don't you remember? You promised to take the second watch and I'm so tired,' Rosie pleaded.

'I didn't promise anything.'

'You did, please, Clara.'

'Don't whine.'

'Little's still out. Get up, please, Clara.'

Finally Clara stirred and felt for her bedroom slippers with one foot while her hand reached for her dressing gown.

'I'm just going out to see Little. Andy takes over at four thirty.' Rosie slipped from the room and almost fell down the stairs to the kitchen. She found her boots and an old coat of Mum's before shooting back the old-fashioned bolts and unfastening the heavy chain on the back door, then slipping out into the night. The cold was biting. Little stood dozing by the high hedge along the edge of the top meadow. He looked quite safe. Everything was silent except for the ducks chattering quietly to one another in the duck house, and a sound of munching coming from the barn. Only a few more hours until daylight, thought Rosie, going back towards the house, and maybe tomorrow the weather will change.

Kelly was waiting for her in the kitchen. He sniffed her bare feet as she took off her boots and he licked her hand. And then sleep engulfed Rosie as soon as her head touched the pillow.

Clara saw nothing to alarm her. Half way through her watch, she went downstairs to fill a hot water bottle. Then the chilblains on her feet started to itch unbearably and by four thirty her teeth were chattering. 'Never again', she vowed, going to Andy's room, finding him already awake. He had set Greyey, his ancient grey alarm clock which only worked when lying on its face.

'Anything happened?' he asked.

'Nothing, absolutely nothing. It's all been an utter waste of time,' complained Clara.

'If we weren't keeping watch, something *would* happen; it's always like that,' said Andy, pulling on socks before slipping his thickest jersey over his head.

'That's a stupid thing to say,' snapped Clara. 'And I personally don't intend to sit up night after night. Soon it will be school again. The whole idea is mad.'

Andy sat on the high-backed chair and wished he could paint. What a picture it would make, he thought — snow-clad roofs, the high hedge round the top field, the trees like sleeping giants. The night before now seemed weeks ago. The beast is not going to come tonight, thought Andy, whatever he is, cat or dog, lion or bear. Perhaps he does not exist at all, perhaps he's been invented by the press or is a man who sucks the blood from sheep. Perhaps the monster we thought we saw was something cooked up by our imagination, after all things like that do happen in the snow. People go mad in snow, blind; they give up and die. He was cold now and went back to his room to fetch a blanket which he put over his shoulders. And then he thought of Tansy killed and eaten in the snow, and he thought that the red stain left behind was the saddest thing he had ever seen. And slowly the moonlight faded and dawn arrived grey and threatening, with a new wind which made the branches on the trees creak like old doors opening.

Bronwen came up the twisty attic stairs in her shabby red dressing gown saying, 'I've brought you a mug of tea. Go back to bed. Did you stay up all night?'

'We took shifts. Mine was the last,' replied Andy, taking the tea. 'But nothing happened. It's awful waiting for something to happen, isn't it? When do you think the beast will strike again, Mum?'

'I hope never.'

'Little has been out all night. We must catch him today,' Andy said. 'No animal must stay out.'

'Your teeth are chattering. Go to bed. I will fetch you a hot water bottle,' said Bronwen.

'I don't want anything else killed. I can't bear it,' replied Andy, returning to his room, thin and somehow beaten in appearance.

And he's too young to look like that, thought Bronwen. She turned downstairs again to coax the Raeburn back to life, to feed Kelly and wake David, her heart suddenly heavy.

All that day everything seemed to be waiting again. The animals stayed locked in, so that Andy remarked, 'This place is becoming a prison. It isn't the same any more.'

They caught Little at lunchtime and later, when they were drinking coffee, there was a tremendous rapping on the door. Clara nearly jumped out of her skin, and Andy said, 'Police. It must be the police again.'

'It can't be,' replied Bronwen, going to the door, while Kelly got out of his basket, lazily, as though saying, 'I had better be ready if I'm needed.' And Rosie thought 'What now for heaven's sake?'

There were three men outside the door. 'Where is he?' asked the largest, who wore a cap on one side of his head, and socks turned down over the top of his boots and a coat which must have known better days.

'Do you mean David? He's only been gone a few

minutes. He just went to see whether the shop was open,' Bronwen said.

Another man was looking into the kitchen now. He had a long nose and eyes like a weasel's and ginger-coloured hair.

'He's in here,' he said.

'He's gone to the shop,' insisted Bronwen.

'We don't mean your 'usband, we mean the dog, we've come for the dog,' said the third man, who was much older with two day's beard on a red face. 'We want to eliminate your dog, that's what we've come for. Three sheep were killed last night and we saw a dog – your dog—'

'He was in here all night,' said Rosie, putting her hand through Kelly's wide studded collar.

'We want to eliminate 'im. We're going to elim-inate all the dogs until the killing stops. We want to put them away for good!'

'You're crazy,' said Bronwen, 'Go away or I will call the police.'

'We'll get 'im anyway,' said the man with the weasel face. 'We know where 'e is now, 'is days are numbered, madam.'

Rosie pulled Kelly into the scullery and shut the door. She could hear the men going now, making threatening noises as they left, promising to come back to get Kelly in the end, and their words echoed in Rosie's head like hammers ringing out the words, 'We'll get 'im in the end.'

'It's all right, they've gone,' said Bronwen a

minute later. 'You can come out, they were half drunk,' but her voice was shaking as she held the door open. 'You mustn't be intimidated.'

'I knew they were drunk,' said Clara.

'There is no work, so they get drunk,' said Bronwen.

'But they meant what they said,' insisted Andy. 'Do you think Kelly's got a double?'

'Definitely not,' said Bronwen. 'Stop worrying. It was just a bunch of men with nothing better to do . . . and drunk into the bargain.' She opened the door to look for David and now they could all see that it was snowing again.

'I wish it would stop. I never want to see snow again. I hate it,' cried Rosie. 'And those men meant what they said.'

'The forecast says we're in for a lot more snow,' said Bronwen, trying to sound calm and matter of fact. 'So you had better do the mucking out before it gets too deep, and, by the way, you left the tools out.'

They swilled their mugs in the sink, wrapped themselves up in layers of clothes. None of them felt much like talking. There was nothing but snow now as far as the eye could see. We'll be cut off again, thought Rosie. It's only the second of January; it can stay like this for two months, decided Bronwen, while Clara felt caged, shut in like an animal, for somehow snow diminished everything, brought the horizon nearer, made the buildings appear lower, imprisoned them all in a world of whiteness. Andy wished that it would go away, just simply in the night, and that the beast would go too, so that they would wake up next morning and know they were safe, all of them including Kelly. But it's too much to hope for, he decided, knocking snow off a fork.

Emma was already mucking out, wearing a skiing outfit which made Clara feel like a pauper in her old overcoat tied round the middle with a broken stirrup leather. Mum said clothes did not matter; it was what you were inside that counted, but grooming Bramble, Clara knew she was wrong. People judge you by your clothes whatever Mum says, she thought.

The ponies were restless; Bramble stood on Clara's feet, Caspar hit Andy in his face with his nose; Lapwing kept trying to barge past the wheelbarrow and escape into the yard. Clara held her foot and cried quietly with despair, not only because her foot hurt, but also because of the injustices of life which gave Emma beautiful clothes and a smart pony and herself nothing but an endless struggle.

Andy sang loudly to keep his spirits up and in an attempt to ignore his aching face. Rosie tied Lapwing to a ring in the wall while she finished cleaning out his loosebox. The day seemed to have been a very long one, without shape, beginning or end. And we must sit up tonight too, thought Rosie, before Emma called, 'Come here, will you. I think Large has got something wrong with her, she's sweating.'

Normally Large stood next to Little, emphasising the different size of a Shire and a Shetland. She was very kind, with a long splash of white down her face, a pink muzzle and two white socks behind. Now she was lying down with wild eyes and swishing tail.

'It could be Azoturia of course,' suggested Emma, opening the box door. 'You know, Monday morning disease. She should have been walked out. They all should have been, we should have cleared a space . . .'

Rosie thought, surely nothing else can go wrong? Haven't we had our share of disaster? Can't we have one day off from disaster?

'What can we do?' she asked, kneeling beside Large in the straw.

'I'm not a vet,' said Emma, holding out a piece of bread which Large refused, fuelling their anxiety still further.

'She's sweating. Feel her ears,' said Rosie.

'We need a vet, don't we?' asked Andy, while Clara cried, 'Why do these things happen to us? We try so hard. Why are we so unlucky?'

'I'll try her with oats,' said Andy, running to the feed shed. But oats did not interest her either.

'If you have animals you have trouble,' replied Emma, quoting her father.

'I'll tell Mum,' Andy said.

Soon Bronwen appeared with VETERINARY NOTES FOR HORSEOWNERS under her arm, saying, 'I've looked up Azoturia and it doesn't sound as though she's got that, Emma, because it appears after exercise and you say she was sweating in her box.' And Clara was pleased that Emma was wrong for once. 'We've rung the vet and he says it sounds like colic,' continued Mum. 'He says to give her a bran mash with Epsom salts in it and to keep her moving. He doesn't think he can get through.'

'She'll twist a gut,' Emma said. 'I'll get a head collar.'

Dad had returned now, covered in snow. He stood looking at Large as Rosie slipped a head collar over her ears recalling that she usually needed a box to stand on. Then they all pulled on the rope and the enormous mare struggled to her feet with a great sigh, before starting to lash out with her large round hoofs in all directions. Dad opened the door, took hold of the head collar rope, and shouted 'Whoa mare, take it easy, steady still.'

'Can a horse die of colic?' asked Rosie.

'I don't know,' said Mum.

'Yes of course,' said Emma, who knew everything. 'And they die in agony.'

'Shall I try the vet again?' asked Andy.

Large proved impossible to manage outside. She kept trying to go down, then slipping on the old cobbles which were hard packed with icy snow. Rosie ran indoors with bran in a bucket, while Dad put Large back in her loose box and Andy ran to the road to see whether the vet was on his way.

'There's not a sign of him, not a car to be seen.

Why can't he come by helicopter?' demanded Andy, running into the kitchen a few minutes later.

'Well she's not dying, not yet anyway,' said Rosie, pouring boiling water on to bran.

'You had better put some chopped carrots in it, or she won't eat the mash. She wouldn't eat bread or oats, so why do you think she'll eat a mash?' asked Andy.

'Stop being so pessimistic,' shouted Rosie, stirring the mash with a wooden spoon.

'What else should I be?' asked Andy. 'First these awful men came, then this happens, and there's sure to be a third thing.'

'Yes, Kelly killed. Do you think I haven't thought about it?' grunted Rosie.

7

Still no vet

'He won't get through. Nothing on wheels can get through,' said Andy, returning to the yard.

'I know. I'm going for an old chap in the village. He was once a horseman,' Dad said.

'What's that?'

'A sort of witch vet, like a witch doctor. They say he could tame the wildest horse with a toad's breast bone,' Dad said.

Large was lying down again, her breath coming too quickly, her eyes glazed. Clara was kneeling beside her.

'He won't be any good. Why can't the vet come by helicopter?' asked Andy.

'Because he can't; a helicopter costs hundreds of pounds to hire and we can't afford it,' Dad answered. 'Even if it *were* possible.'

'I'll come with you then,' said Andy, who could not bear to look at Large now. He wanted to do something if only to keep his mind off twisted guts and Large dying.

'A horseman should mean a rider,' he insisted, following Dad.

'Yes, I know, but it means something different here. It means someone who understands horses, who doesn't need a vet,' said Dad.

'Was he around when there were no vets?' asked Andy. 'Is he very old?'

'In his eighties, I think.'

'How do you know about him?'

'I met him in the pub.'

'What's his name?'

'Bert Hayman.'

'Do you think those men will really kill Kelly?'

'Not if we keep him in.'

'All the time? Day and night?'

'More or less.'

'Poor Kelly . . .'

The snow on the road reached to their knees.

'Why don't they send a snow plough to clear it?' demanded Andy angrily.

'They've probably cleared the main road. This is only a minor one.'

'What about the farmers? Why don't they do it?'

'They're all old round here,' Dad said. 'Here we are. Be on your best behaviour, Andy.'

They had reached a line of old cottages. Bert Hayman had cleared the path to his crooked front door and was standing in his kitchen skinning a rabbit. His cottage smelt of burning wood and of tobacco. There were no carpets or rugs on the floors and not much furniture either.

'What can I do for you?' he asked, laying down his knife.'

He was small, with eyes like an eagle's staring from beneath bushy grey eyebrows. He looked twisted, like a tree which has stood all its life in a wind straight from the sea.

'We can't get a vet. We've got a mare with colic. We will make it worth your while. Can you help?' said Dad.

'Please,' added Andy. 'Otherwise she'll die. She's got it badly, Mr Hayman.'

Bert Hayman put on his coat. It was a very big coat with many pockets in it. 'You said colic, did you? Wait a minute while I get a drench,' he said.

'He doesn't look educated,' said Andy, in a low voice. 'I don't think he'll be any good. I wish the vet would come.'

'Well he can't so that's that,' snapped Dad, and Andy saw now that he was taut too, like tight-stretched wire.

'I'm ready,' said Bert Hayman, pushing ancient bottles into the pockets of his coat.

Back in the yard, Large was down lying on her side with her legs stretched out, so that Clara could not help shouting, 'She's dying. I know she is. Do something someone.'

Rosie had offered the mare the mash, but it had

been refused immediately. Bronwen had put a hot water bottle in a case shaped like a rabbit against her side where it looked minute and useless. Emma had fetched coffee in a thermos. It was real percolated coffee which Rosie hated.

Snow had started to fall again, in tiny flakes. And somehow along the way time had ceased to exist, for lunchtime had come and gone and no one had noticed.

Hurrying along the road, Andy wished that Bert Hayman could walk a little faster. He was talking to Dad now about Kelly, telling him to keep him inside under lock and key. 'Otherwise you won't see him no more,' he said.

Andy expected everything to be different when he reached the yard. He had prayed as he walked to a God he hardly believed in to make Large better, but she was just the same, worse even. God had done nothing.

'She's going to die, isn't she?' he asked no one in particular, himself perhaps, or God?

Bert slipped into the loose box silently like a burglar into a house at night. He squatted on the straw breathing into the mare's nose and after a few minutes she stood up, her legs trembling, her sides strewn with straw.

'I need you to help me,' said Bert Hayman to Dad. 'And I may need a twitch.'

'A twitch?'

'Don't you know what a twitch is?'

'No. Does anyone?' asked Dad looking round, his fair hair wet with melting snow, his cheeks unusually red and glistening.

'Yes, and it's horrible. It's cruel,' cried Emma. 'There's a row of them in the forge but Jim the blacksmith never uses them.'

'Give me some twine and a bit of wood and somethin' to stand on. We'll see if we can manage without the twitch, but I want one just in case. These are my last drenches. We can't afford to waste them, guv'nor. There's no more where they came from,' said Bert Hayman, taking off his coat and rolling up his sleeves. He put the head collar rope over a beam which ran the length of what had once been a cart shed, then added twine to it. 'You look strong, hang on to it. Pull when I'm in the box. We want the mare's head 'igh otherwise the drench won't run down her throat,' he told Rosie. 'And you, guv'nor, get the other side of the mare and 'old 'er tongue.'

But the big mare was having none of it. She was too strong for Rosie to hold; she used her head like a battering ram, and kicked out with her hind hoofs. Dad was knocked off the old beer crate he had fetched for himself to stand on. Rosie's hands were cut by the twine. Even Bert Hayman was sent sprawling in the straw. ''Ere give me some more twine and a bit of wood, that's right, an axe handle will do,' he said, struggling up, looking at Emma with venomous eyes, so that she shrank back against the door. He twisted the twine round the mare's upper lip, put the wood through the twine and twisted it tighter. It was all accomplished in seconds, while Clara hid her eyes and Emma stood outside in the piercing cold muttering, 'It's barbaric, inhumane, diabolical.'

'It's better than dying, isn't it?' Bert Hayman asked no one in particular, climbing on his box again, while Dad, climbing on his, took hold of the twitch and Rosie pulled on the twine attached to the head collar rope, and Clara thought that it looked like a scene from a medieval torture chamber.

The ancient cork had been drawn from the bottle, the concoction ran slowly down the mare's throat. She did not move, only her eyes and hunched quarters showing her fear and dislike.

'She'll be better now,' said Bert Hayman, getting down. 'You can let her go now Rosie, and you can let go the twitch, guv'nor. I'll need a wash though.' His bare arms were covered with drench, and he looked small and old, his back bent from years of toil, his hands misshapen by it. Dad handed him his coat. 'If she isn't better in 'alf an 'our, she'll need another one,' said Bert Hayman, struggling into his coat. 'Do you think you can manage?'

'No. We can't,' said Mum firmly. 'Come in the warm.'

Bert Hayman patted the mare before he left. She seemed quite calm now and unresentful.

'The snow will be gone by Tuesday, you'll see,'

he said, smiling at Rosie, showing his one remaining tooth. 'There won't be none left by Tuesday.'

'How do you know?' asked Andy.

'That's my secret . . .'

He walked slowly so as not to slip; then, looking round him, said, 'You've made a lot of changes. I worked 'ere when I was a boy. Up 'ere every mornin' I was, four o'clock, to get the 'orses ready to go out in the fields. Different it was then, different world, different altogether.'

'Times change,' said Dad.

'Not for the better, they don't,' replied Bert Hayman.

'He says the same thing over and over again, and he smells. He's awful. Wherever did Dad find him, Andy?' asked Clara.

'In the cottages. But look, she's better already. Look, she's relaxing,' Andy cried. 'Dad says he's like a witch doctor.'

'He smells of all sorts of awful things,' complained Clara again.

'Of dead rabbits and toad's breast bones, and of strange potions,' said Andy.

'I believe you like him,' complained Clara.

'She's nibbling at the mash. Look! She's going to be all right,' Rosie said. 'Oh isn't it wonderful? She isn't going to die after all.'

'I'm going home. It's long past lunchtime,' said Emma. 'I'm glad she's better, but I still think the twitch wasn't necessary and I hate the old man. I bet he was terrible to horses in the olden days.'

'And I bet he wasn't,' shouted Andy.

'You like him then?'

'I didn't say that, but I respect him and if he saves Large's life I shall be grateful to him for ever.'

'The vet would have given her an injection. It would have been so civilised by comparison,' Emma said. 'I bet he docked horses without anaesthetics when he was young.'

'But the vet couldn't come, idiot,' shouted Andy.

'I'll be back in the afternoon to walk out Sandpiper. See if you can clear some of the snow by then, will you?' asked Emma.

'Yes madam,' shouted Andy.

'She's eating properly. Look! It's like a miracle,' Rosie said. 'I simply don't believe it . . .'

Bert Hayman drank two cans of beer and wiping his mouth on the back of his hand, said, 'I'll just take another look at the mare. She should be better now.'

He had brought snow into the house on his boots and the snow had turned to water and, when he left, his smell lingered. But in spite of the twitch Large rubbed her nose on Bert Hayman's shoulder when she saw him. She looked peaceful now.

'It may be spasmodic,' Bert Hayman said, looking at Dad. 'You'll have to watch 'er. I'll leave the second bottle with you. Drench her if she's in pain again. I can't do more.'

'And we can't thank you enough,' said Dad, putting a five pound note into his horny palm, from where it swiftly vanished into a pocket in his coat.

'You've been wonderful,' Mum said. 'You've saved her life.'

Bert Hayman called the mare, 'Gal', as he stroked her neck and felt her ears, saying, 'You'll be all right now then.'

'What caused it?' asked Mum.

'Too much feed and not enough movement,' he answered promptly. ''Orses need exercise regular.'

'Watch your dog, don't forget now,' he said before departing, an ancient figure, seeming as old as the trees which stood by the gate and as ancient as the tools in the Victorian kitchen, which he had probably used in the past.

'Meeting him is like going back in history,' said Dad. 'I wonder how old he is?'

'He wasn't born this century, that's certain,' replied Mum.

And Rosie wondered what it felt like to be so old, to have lived in the days before cars existed, when all cows were still milked by hand, and the farm buildings held rows of horses.

'Anyway Large is saved. Now we have only the beast to deal with,' said Dad.

'And the ponies to lead out. We had better stop giving them oats from now on,' Rosie said.

'There won't be any snow left by Tuesday, Mr Hayman said so. We'll be able to ride again, to catch the bus and go shopping, to spend our Christmas money,' cried Andy.

'It feels as though the snow has been here for ever. Do you remember how we loved it when we lived in the town. It was wonderful then, like fairyland,' said Clara.

They led the ponies out one by one; putting them back in their boxes with snow-packed hoofs. Rosie could not believe that the snow would ever go, that the fields could ever be green again and the trees free of snow. A wind was blowing now, a wild angry wind which made her shiver; the sort of wind which screams in the night and whips off dustbin lids like a devil, which sends slates toppling off roofs, and trees crashing to the ground. The wind worried Rosie, though she could not have said why; it seemed an ill omen, another trial to be survived. It made the ponies nervous, so that they stood at the backs of their boxes with pricked ears, listening. It blew the snow into drifts making Rosie remember the night of the blizzard, filling her with a burst of sudden anxiety. And she did not like the wind for another reason, because it made everything harder, toppling wheelbarrows and banging doors. Clara had already found an excuse to go indoors, was sitting now listening to the wind howling, wishing that she was in Bermuda or the South of France, wishing they were rich enough to fly away every winter to somewhere warm. She considered her parents hopeless, almost despised them, longed for parents who had parties, cupboards full of drinks, a car which others envied. She looked at her broken nails and saw that her fingers were cracking at the corners. When I'm eighteen I shall go to America and never return, she thought.

The wind made Kelly restless. He hated being kept in the house. He was always at the back door now asking to go out. He could not understand why he had suddenly become a prisoner, why he could not run free any more. He was never happy now.

Bronwen was preparing a meal. It was neither lunch nor tea but a mixture of the two. Food was beginning to run out. The lights were still on outside. Marigold had to be milked, but David was already shutting in the fowls for the night, bolting doors top and bottom, and Large was eating hay now, relaxed except for the wind.

'Shall we shut all the doors top and bottom tonight, Dad?' asked Andy.

'Yes.'

'Emma says it will make Sandpiper cough,' announced Rosie, laden with hay nets.

'Damn Emma,' said Dad.

The ducks were quacking softly now. Like people before they go to sleep thought Rosie who loved the ducks for their cheerfulness. The goats still needed feeding; the sheep and pigs were settled for the night. In spite of the snow and the wind, it was warm in the old farm buildings. The two outdoor cats had settled in the granary for the night. Then

Mum came out with a bucket to milk Marigold. 'There's a meal waiting inside,' she said.

'Where's Clara?' asked Dad.

'Sitting by the fire. She says she's got a sore throat.'

They all knew Clara's sore throats which came and went to order, which disappeared when all the work was done.

Emma now appeared saying, 'Please don't shut Sandpiper's door. I don't want him coughing in the morning. Horses need masses of air.'

'As you like. He's your horse,' Dad said.

'Do you think the beast will come tonight?' asked Andy, bolting the barn's massive doors.

'I couldn't say. But there's no need to sit up,' Dad said.

But Rosie knew she would not sleep, not deeply anyway, not until the beast had gone or been killed.

'The wind's getting worse every minute,' Emma said.

'Thank God we're not at sea,' replied Dad.

The wind made them edgy and it almost blew Mum over when she appeared from the cowshed carrying a pail of milk. 'Remember to switch the lights off, David,' she said, going towards the house.

'Why don't you leave them on; it might frighten the beast,' suggested Emma.

'That's not a bad idea,' said Dad.

'Like lighting a camp fire to keep wolves at bay,' said Andy. 'I'll just check Large again.'

Mum had found her a blanket and sewn braid on it. She looked very peaceful munching hay; she blew hot air down Andy's neck and nuzzled his hair.

Mum was calling now from the house . . . 'It's getting late. Hurry up, there's crumpets.'

They had to push Kelly out of the way to get inside. 'Great slob. Why's he always in the way?' asked Mum.

'He's unhappy,' Rosie said quickly. 'He feels rejected.'

The kitchen smelt of fried bacon, and of smoke, because the wind was blowing down the chimney. Sometimes they could hear the coal hissing as snow fell on it.

The old windows were rattling too and Mum had stuffed bits of cloth under the doors to keep the cold out.

'Sometimes I wish we were back in the town. Life seems so hard, David,' she said now.

'So do I,' agreed Clara. 'Just look at my hands.'

'You couldn't have ponies,' said Dad.

'But we could have other things,' Clara said.

'Listen to the wind. I've never heard such a wind before,' Mum said, putting food on plates. 'It sounds like the sea. I feel as though we are on an island in the middle of an ocean.'

'It must drop soon, and at least the animals are all under cover,' Dad said.

Then one of the doors upstairs slammed, making them all jump. Kelly lay with his nose against the back door, whining.

'He doesn't get enough exercise,' Rosie said, making excuses for him because she could sense Mum's exasperation and growing dislike of the big dog which had to be kept in like a prisoner.

'He eats as much as two people. Do you think spring will ever come?' Mum asked.

'In three months' time,' replied Dad, laughing.

'I don't think I can survive that long,' Mum answered and Rosie saw again how tired she was. 'And the food is running out. Do you think you can get to the shop tomorrow, David?'

'I don't see why not.'

'If you can't there's nothing but baked beans and potatoes left and, of course, milk.'

'You know I'm allergic to milk,' said Clara. 'And I can't stand baked beans.'

'The hens' corn is getting low too,' Dad said.

'Must we be so dismal?' cried Andy.

'Listen!' cried Mum. 'There goes a tree. I hope it isn't an oak.' The crash of the tree was deafening, louder than the wind. They ran outside to look. Andy's favourite oak was lying across the drive, its mighty trunk split asunder.

'Not to worry, I'll clear it first thing,' said Dad quickly.

'We really are cut off now,' said Mum.

The oak was enormous, its branches stretched in

all directions. The wind whipped snow into their faces and slammed the back door shut.

'I loved that tree,' shouted Andy. 'I tell you I loved it.'

'It will be fine by morning,' Dad announced. 'You'll be able to sunbathe, Clara.'

'Don't be mad, Dad,' Clara said.

They sat by the Raeburn listening to the wind. It was not a nice sound. Andy imagined himself at sea, the waves lashing the decks, the wind screaming. He imagined the ship keeling over. He got up and started to pace the room.

'What's the matter?'

'I don't know. I'm upset about the oak. It was such a lovely old tree and I feel scared suddenly,' Andy said.

'It's because we are still town people in our bones,' suggested Mum.

'And always will be,' exclaimed Clara.

'Shut up. I'm not, and never will be,' cried Rosie.

The lights flickered; the telephone tinkled; Kelly whined. Soot fell down the chimney with a thud, putting out the fire in the Raeburn. Then the lights went out.

8

I knew it was Kelly

They tripped over one another looking for torches and candles while outside they could hear branches falling; then water started to drip slowly through the roof.

'God what a night! Telephone the electricity people,' cried Mum. But the telephone had gone dead again.

Soon three candles were on the table. Dad was trying to get the Raeburn alight and Mum had put a bucket under the drip.

'I wanted to watch television tonight. It's my favourite programme. Someone do something. I can't miss it; I've been looking forward to it for ages,' cried Clara.

'There's nothing to be done, love,' replied Dad, his hands sooty.

'I want to go back. I want to go back to the town; this house is full of spiders,' cried Clara.

'You liked it in the summer,' Andy told her, severely. 'And you like the money you can earn helping with teas. There are no jobs in town.'

Kelly was whining again, pacing the room, getting in everyone's way. He had hardly been out for three days. Snow was driven against the windows by the wind, which blew so hard that sometimes the whole house shook.

'We had better go to bed. Everything must be better in the morning.' Dad said, suddenly sounding resigned.

'It's early; it's only seven o'clock. Won't television come on later? What are the men doing? We can't go to bed at seven o'clock,' cried Clara.

'The candles won't last for ever, and nor will my torch,' Dad answered. 'And you must each have a candle to take to bed with you.'

'Can't I go to Emma's? She's got a colour television.'

'Look out of the window,' Dad said. 'Go on, look.'

Clara looked. Everything was in darkness; not a light on anywhere.

'See what I mean?'

'It feels like the olden days. I bet Bert Hayman is managing all right,' Andy said.

'Shall I take a look at Large?' suggested Rosie.

'We haven't enough battery left in my torch,' Dad answered.

'Can't we drive the car up? Use the headlights?' suggested Andy.

'And get stuck. She's all right,' Dad said.

They sat looking at each other like conspirators, while Mum washed up, saying that it was easier done alone. 'If you help you're sure to knock over my candle,' she said.

It was cold in the kitchen and getting colder every minute. 'I'll take a hot water bottle to bed with me,' Clara said.

'If the water's hot enough. You can't use the electric kettle,' Mum answered.

'The lights may come on again,' Clara suggested.

'Yes, it's possible, but I doubt it on such a night,' replied Dad. 'What about Emma? She isn't alone, is she?'

'No, her father's at home this week,' Mum answered.

Rosie wondered how they were managing, since the whole house was run on electricity, without even a fireplace in the sitting room.

'It's like the end of the world, isn't it?' she asked.

'If only we had some paraffin we could use the oil lamp from the kitchen next door,' said Mum. 'The one we use as an exhibit. I can remember my old uncle lighting it. He used to trim the wick and clean the glass for hours.'

'I hate hearing about the olden days,' Clara said, restlessly going to the door and back. She felt hemmed in by the semi-darkness and by the snow.

'Go on, go to bed; everything will look different in the morning,' Dad told them. 'I'll get up early when it's light and get the Raeburn going before any of you are up. I'll bring you tea in bed.'

'I hate tea,' retorted Clara.

'Coffee then.'

Their bedrooms were freezing, particularly Andy's at the top of the house. They turned on light switches from habit, but when Rosie looked out of her small lattice window there was still nothing to see, just the wind howling. So presently she crept down to the bottom of her bed, burying her head completely. Andy did not undress but went to bed in jeans and three jerseys. Clara brushed her hair and seeing that she looked beautiful by candlelight, was pleased.

'Blow your candles out, don't forget now. Have you each got a box of matches in case you need to go somewhere in the night?' Mum called, up the stairs.

Rosie could hear Kelly prowling about still. He pads like a wild animal kept captive in a zoo, she thought, and wanted spring to come with a longing she had not experienced before. She imagined the fields green again, the ponies sleek in summer coats, the place crammed with visitors, money pouring in, so that they could all have new clothes, new tack, perhaps a new car. This year it's got to happen, she thought. This year must be a break-through. She saw herself riding to gymkhanas, hacking home with rosettes on Lapwing's bridle, instead of giving pony rides weekend after weekend.

Andy was asleep already, dreaming that Bert

Hayman was in the kitchen making tea, Clara was imagining New York, the lights and crowds, but most of all the lights. We're never going to be rich, she thought, never. I must go it alone; there's no other way. She could hear her parents going to bed now, telling Kelly to go to sleep, 'For God's sake!' Mum's voice suddenly strident, because she was sick of the dog. Dad was calmer, because he had bought him in the first place, had brought him home as a guard dog, and so could not admit that he was useless.

'It's not snowing any more, David,' Mum said. 'I think the worst is over. Listen, the wind has dropped.'

'I hope you're right,' Dad said.

Then Clara fell asleep wearing her thickest nightie with bedsocks on her feet. Andy went on dreaming about Bert Hayman and Rosie lay wishing she had a torch because she wanted to read, and slowly the wind dropped and everything became still outside.

Rosie was dreaming that a war had started, there were tanks everywhere and bombers diving low over the farm buildings, and the animals were screaming in a wild terrified chorus. Then suddenly she knew that though the tanks and bombers were a dream, the screams were real. She fell out of bed, pulled on jeans, a pullover, a coat. She shouted, 'Wake up, everyone.' At the same moment she heard the crash of breaking glass downstairs; then she was running down the stairs still calling, 'Wake up, wake up,' her eyes blurred with sleep. She could hear the guinea fowl shrieking now, the geese warning of danger, the chickens squawking, the peacocks screaming, and somewhere in the midst of it all, a pony neighing. She could hear the others getting up now, Dad shouting, 'Are the lights on? Where's my gun?' She slid back the bolts on the back door, pulling on her boots as she looked on a landscape so still that it was impossible to believe that there had ever been a gale blowing. The night was starlit now, the stars like jewels in the dark velvet sky, the fallen tree like a fallen giant touched with silver by the moon. Then she could see Kelly in the distance, giving tongue, and her heart started to race wildly as she ran to the stable.

The hens were still cackling as she found a head collar and by the sound of it there was bedlam inside the barn. But there was no blood, no corpse yet to be seen. She vaulted on to a surprised Lapwing, pushed him through the snow with her legs as she heard the others emerging from the house calling, 'Where are you going? What's happened?'

'I'm going after Kelly,' she yelled.

'Not him again. He's broken the window in the kitchen. It must be the moon which sets him off, he must be destroyed this time,' Mum shouted.

And Dad said, 'I've got my gun.'

The wind had swept the slope beyond the top meadow clear of snow. Kelly was still giving tongue and Rosie could see other lights moving across the fields now; then someone fired a gun, then another and another and then Rosie was riding towards the hedge which divided the top field from the fields beyond, from the arable and the plough. She had never jumped so high before and Lapwing's hoofs were full of snow; but there was no turning back now – another few minutes and Kelly could be dead. Her legs drummed against Lapwing's sides, he took off, cleared the hedge, then floundering in the snow drift on the other fell, while Rosie clutching frantically to his mane, cried, 'Stand up. Help. Help.'

'I knew it was Kelly. I knew it all along,' Mum was saying. Mum who was nearly always right about everything. 'And if he's killed something tonight, we will have to pay, David. We will have to pay for all the earlier deaths too, you realize that, don't you, David?'

But David wasn't listening. He was wishing that he had a two two rifle instead of a shotgun.

Andy had a hatchet in his hand, while Clara was still pulling on boots, knowing that she would never keep up with the others, already thinking of turning back. And somewhere, not far away, a tractor was starting up, motor bikes and landrovers. And they could all see now that the gale had swept large areas free of snow leaving it in drifts against hedges and barns, so that now even a landrover could cross the fields in places.

'The house will be even colder with the window broken,' wailed Clara, running across the yard. It's Monday, Andy remembered, and Bert Hayman said that the snow would be gone by Tuesday.

In the new houses Emma was looking out, woken by the commotion. I had better check on Sandpiper, she thought, and pulled on her clothes. Her father slept soundly in the next room, because he was not tuned to hear the cry of animals in distress, only to the shriek of the telephone or to the sound of letters dropping on to the synthetic mat by the front door.

Emma found a torch, gloves, a hood for her head, and a warm scarf for her neck. She put on fur boots, and because she was well organised, it only took a few minutes; then she was outside listening to the Wells family calling to one another, the cries of the animals growing less as the danger they feared retreated, the shouts of Rosie half buried in the drift and, in the distance, the sound of Kelly still giving tongue. She ran towards the stables calling, 'What's happened? Why are you up?'

And Bronwen answered, 'It's Kelly. He's got out; he's hunting. He must be the monster after all.' And she was crying.

Lapwing was out of the drift now, and the fields in

front were almost clear of snow. Rosie patted him, saying, 'You're wonderful, the best ever,' before vaulting on again and pushing him on across the harsh winter landscape. The hedges were banked with snow, the trees bold and majestic, with nothing to be seen close by, not even a rabbit – though farther away people were converging from all directions on Kelly. Kelly who was still giving tongue, his voice echoing across the landscape telling everyone where he was, signing his own death warrant, thought Rosie. In her imagination she saw him lying dead; the farmers standing round, congratulating themselves; Mum's anger; Dad's tired resolute face as he said, 'I know I'm responsible. You will all receive compensation.' And it will ruin us, she thought. Yet she knew too, because of the sequence of events, because she had heard the animals screaming in fear before the window broke, that it could not be Kelly, and because of that she must be there first, before the tractors, the running figures and the landrover in the distance. She knew that almost everyone would be armed to the teeth, and she could feel fear mounting inside her, making her legs weak just when she needed them strong to urge Lapwing faster. Lapwing was a Highland pony, so he could cross the terrain more easily than a thoroughbred, the snow balling less in his sturdy hoofs. And yet they were not gaining on Kelly, not a metre, not a centimetre, in fact he seemed to be growing more distant all the time. Then Rosie thought that the farmers must have been sitting up listening. Or was it their dogs who heard the noise and relayed it from farm to farm, each dog warning the next one?

Then she thought that really it did not matter how they knew. All that mattered now was to get to Kelly before they killed him.

Lapwing was sweating in his thick winter coat, which had seemed to grow centimetres more since the blizzard. He was blowing too.

Then suddenly there was silence. Kelly had stopped giving tongue and had reached his quarry, whatever it was. And that filled Rosie with terror too.

The others were running; Dad in the lead, the others following, their legs already aching, their boots weighed down with snow. In the yard Emma checked the animals, seeing that each one was still alive, calming Sandpiper who was missing Lapwing. Although the animals were quiet now, they were not at peace, but listening, their eyes apprehensive, their quarters hunched, the ponies moving round and round their boxes. Suddenly the yard had ceased to be a happy place and become fearful. And all because of Kelly presumably. Or was there another killer abroad? Two perhaps? wondered Emma.

Soon her father approached, calling, 'Whatever are you doing out at this hour, Emma? Have you taken leave of your senses?' His hair, which was just turning grey, was standing up around his head, his town shoes slipped in the snow, his black overcoat looked out of place amid the farm buildings.

'Didn't you hear the commotion? All hell was let loose. The monster's been. Look, there are paw-marks,' cried Emma, bending down. 'Look!'

Rosie could see Kelly clearly now. He was fighting, trying to kill something as big as himself. A deer perhaps, she thought, a calf, a ewe, but what would they be doing out on such a night? Lapwing was tiring. Unexercised for almost a week, he was far from fit, and the sweat from his sides stung Rosie through her jeans. And now far away in the East dawn was breaking, stealing slowly across the sky, grey and pink, a new day beginning, a day which was destined to be unforgettable.

9

'Don't shoot'

Rosie was thinking of the men who had called to kill Kelly. Were they approaching now? Wouldn't they shoot first and ask questions afterwards? And supposing it wasn't Kelly who was guilty and they shot him? It would be worse then. If he was not guilty, it would be murder.

Suddenly her thoughts were just a wild jumble, a jigsaw. She could see Kelly more clearly now, and that the scattered snow around him was turning red. She began to shout then, 'Kelly, stop it, Stop it, Kelly. Come here, Kelly'; to whistle through half frozen lips while a rush of tears cascaded down her face. Lapwing would not go forward, terrified by the fight and the smell of blood, and there was nothing to tie him to, and nothing to hit him with either. Her legs thudding wildly against his sides did not move him a centimetre, so that in the end she simply leapt off, leaving him to turn round and make for home, his heavy Highland tail trailing behind him.

'Kelly. Come here, please Kelly.' His jaws dripped blood, his face ran with it. He had taken a terrible battering but was still fighting – fighting an animal which was black, whose eyes showed green when you could see them, an animal as quick as a cat or a tiger, an animal fighting for its life. And suddenly Rosie thought, it's a lion and it's going to kill Kelly; it's killing him now and there's no hope. She started to shout, 'Stop it, Kelly . . .' but to no avail. Then she looked for a stick, but there was not a tree in sight, not a hedge even. And all the time people were bearing down on her . . .

And now there was a gaping wound in Kelly's shoulder, so deep that she could see the bone showing through . . . and his soft gun dog mouth ran with a river of blood.

'Don't shoot, David, you'll shoot Rosie. Can't you see she's there,' shouted Bronwen.

'I'm not a fool.' They were running across ploughed land now, their breath coming in gasps. Lapwing had just galloped past, his dun sides drenched with sweat. 'Let him go. He won't hurt,' Dad had said, loading his gun as he ran.

'We must get there first,' shouted Andy. 'We mustn't let the farmers kill Kelly.'

They could see the tractors and landrover converging, their lights blazing, all packed with men eager for the kill. They could hear dogs yapping, men calling to one another, their blood up, their voices high with excitement. And in that state they are capable of anything, thought Andy. Then they could see that Rosie had taken off her boots and was frantically beating at the two animals rolling in deadly embrace on the frozen earth, their jaws locked together, and Dad shouted, 'It's a puma. Stand back, Rosie. Get out of the way. Move.'

He fired twice, then twice again, and running towards him Rosie screamed, 'You've killed them both, you fool, Dad. You've killed Kelly.'

It was a moment they would never forget – the two animals lying there while dawn came and the moonlight faded. Men climbed down from the landrover and tractors. And the three who had appeared only a few days ago threatening to kill Kelly said, 'You haven't killed him, have you? He was a good dog after all. We were wrong about him.'

Rosie could not stop crying. It was not just for Kelly, it was for everything – the long night, the day of the blizzard, for Large's colic, for the cold farmhouse and the frightened animals, but also because she was limp with exhaustion and disappointment. That Kelly should die just when he had fought the monster was too unjust to bear, too awful to think about.

The men were all talking at once now, saying, 'Is it really a puma? Where did it come from? Not from your place, David?' They were on christian name terms again now, no longer

107

enemies threatening to kill Kelly. 'Fancy a puma. Never seen one before. Looks like a tigress don't it,' said weasel face.

Andy turned to his parents. 'How could you do it?' he screamed. 'How could you shoot him, Dad? And *you* never liked him, Mum. You thought it was him all the time and it wasn't. He's a hero, isn't he? He'll have to have a grave with a stone on it.'

'That's right,' cried Clara, arriving at last. 'A stone with a quotation on it. Something beautiful, really beautiful.'

'He was a great dog,' said a man wearing a deer-stalker hat. 'It takes a brave dog to take on a puma, and you can see the mauling he's taken.'

'I always said the monster was a cat of sorts, but I never thought of a puma. What are we going to do with it. Stuff it?' asked Dad.

'You could try. Do you want the skin? Make a nice stole for your missus,' said a man with a beard. 'We can't leave it here anyway. If you don't want it I'll have it, David. And what about the dog? Do you want him buried here?'

'No way,' cried Clara. 'He's coming home with us. He's going to have a proper grave with a stone with his name on it.'

'Oh is he now?' said the man, laughing at her. 'You're going to put flowers on it, are you?'

'Ignore him,' said Andy quickly, seeing the anger in Clara's face.

'Better put the dog in the landrover then,' said

the man. 'Bring him down to your place then, if we can get through.'

'There's a tree down,' said Dad listlessly.

'We'll help you clear it then. You'll get the reward anyway, since it was your dog what pulled it down, and you what shot it, no doubt about that.'

'Yes, two thousand pounds. Didn't you know?'

Dad shook his head. Overcome with grief for having killed Kelly, nothing was really registering any more.

'You'll be able to buy a new dog, a pedigree one this time.'

'We don't want a pedigree one,' said Andy, hating the man, hating everyone.

'A new pony then.'

'We've got enough ponies, thank you,' said Rosie coldly.

They laid out the puma mourning its torn skin and ruined fur. Clara could not bear to look, could not bear to look at either of them – puma or Kelly. Rosie could not see them through her tears. The men went on talking. The children ceased to listen, turned to each other in their grief. Dad went to pick Kelly up, waving the men away. 'Take the tail end, Andy, will you?' he said.

Mum turned to walk down the hill, saying, 'I don't need a lift, thanks all the same.'

Andy wanted to refuse, but not wishing to appear a coward, he gingerly put his hand under Kelly's

109

haunches, then cried, 'Look Dad, he's breathing. He isn't dead. He's still alive.'

'Put him in the landrover then, don't waste time,' shouted the man in the deerstalker. 'Hurry now. I'll take him straight to the vet. Get in, all of you.'

'He can't be alive,' cried Rosie.

'He is,' shouted Andy. 'He's breathing.'

They all piled into the landrover; all except Mum who said she had to milk Marigold because cows could not wait and they might be hours. She was smiling now. Suddenly they were all smiling.

The landrover bumped across the fields while Rosie held Kelly's head. His eyes were closed; his coat was sticky with blood, the bone in his right shoulder gaping through torn flesh. But he was alive. Clara kept stroking him. Andy sat watching his breathing, praying that it would not stop, wishing the landrover would go faster. Dad's face was set. He looked haggard and unshaven in the morning light.

'What about Lapwing?' asked Rosie.

'Your mother will see to him.'

The landrover stuck in drifts and had to be dug out. Twice it nearly spun off the road altogether. Then they met another car with chains on its tyres and had to back up, wheels spinning, and all the time minutes were passing. Kelly lay quite still through it all, hardly breathing so that sometimes they feared he had passed away altogether and would have to be buried after all.

'I jumped the hedge. I never thought I could jump it,' Rosie remembered. 'It must be a metre and a quarter at least.'

'Well done,' said Dad, sitting in the front with the man in the deerstalker, turning to look at the children, his gun on his knees.

'Your blood was up,' the man in the deerstalker said.

'We landed in a drift. I thought we were never going to get out. It was up to Lapwing's withers.'

'Do you think Kelly will live?' asked Andy.

'I don't know . . .'

The vet was still in bed; he had to be fetched from his house. He unlocked the surgery and rang for assistance.

'What about tetanus?' asked Andy.

'Dogs don't get it. We had better X-ray him. He hasn't lost too much blood, but the stitching will take a time.' The vet was half asleep and kept rubbing his eyes.

The children were sent to sit in the waiting room, which was full of advertisements for kittens needing homes and leaflets telling you how to look after your pets.

It was seven thirty now, with daylight spreading across the tarmac outside and the street lamps going out one by one. Rosie nearly went to sleep; Clara's stomach cried out to be fed, and Andy read the leaflets without noticing what he read. Then going to the window Andy said, 'The snow's melting. It's over. We'll be able to ride again.'

'I don't believe you,' Rosie said. 'It's only happening in the town, towns always melt first; they put down salt, that's why.'

'It's melting on the trees, and the gutters are running with water. Come and look,' cried Andy. 'It's a miracle.'

The others joined him and it did seem like a miracle. They put their hands outside and tested the air. 'We won't need gloves,' Andy said.

'I hope the lights are on,' said Clara. 'I want to use my hair drier.'

Dad appeared then, saying, 'We're going home, he's going to be all right. They have to put him to sleep before they can sew him up.'

'He's asleep already,' Andy said.

'That's different. He could wake up.'

The man in the deerstalker was still waiting outside in his landrover. He had bought *The Times* from somewhere and was reading it. He held the doors open for them.

'He's going to be all right,' Dad repeated, climbing in. 'But where did the puma come from, that's what I want to know.'

'People have them as pets, you know,' replied the man in the deerstalker, who turned out to be called Mr Beecroft. 'But no one will claim him, you can be sure of that. You see the farmers are insured against dogs worrying their sheep, but not against pumas. The owner will keep his mouth shut not wanting to pay the damages . . .'

'Poor puma,' said Rosie.

'They make good pets, because they never kill humans, though they can pull down a horse at full gallop,' explained Mr Beecroft, driving through the wakening town. 'They are like big cats. I knew a chap who had one once. It used to sit in an armchair.'

People were taking in milk bottles now, drawing back their curtains, riding to work on bicycles, starting up cars and motor bicycles. A whole night had passed without Andy noticing, and a new day was beginning.

'Where has the puma been taken then?' he asked.

'To the police station.'

'Will we really get two thousand pounds?' asked Clara.

'But of course, and I think it went up some more last week. I think it actually stands at five thousand,' said Mr Beecroft.

The main road was cleared now and the side roads were covered with slush. Everywhere gutters were running with water and trees dripping.

It's like a new beginning, thought Rosie. She leaned forward to her father and asked, 'What will we do with the five thousand pounds, Dad?'

'We haven't got it yet,' Dad said.

'But when we have?'

'We will discuss that later.'

And now they all had their plans. We each should have a thousand, decided Clara. We need a landrover, thought Andy, with a long wheelbase and a hard top. Rosie saw new animals appearing, monkeys, baboons, a black bear from Malaysia. And slowly the sun came out, a watery wintry sun. Then Rosie remembered that Mum at first had thought the beast was a puma, so she was right about that. But wrong about Kelly – and with him lying in the surgery between life and death, that was hard to forgive.

10

'We'll aim for the top'

'I thought pumas were brown,' said Emma.

They were sitting in the kitchen now, celebrating. The lights were on again, the telephone working, the Raeburn alight and, best of all, the sun was shining through the windows.

Rosie had described jumping the hedge half a dozen times before finally saying, 'And I still can't believe it. I really can't.'

And now Dad said, 'They are often black and obviously she had escaped from somewhere.'

'Why did they accuse Kelly, then? He's not like a puma,' said Andy.

'I suppose they *wanted* it to be a dog. And he's black after all,' Dad said. 'That first photo must have been a fake.'

'But he's not the least like a puma,' insisted Andy.

'The eye tends to see what it wants. Your mother said it was a puma, until Kelly was accused,' remembered Dad.

Emma's father had taken a day off work. He looked out of place in the old farmhouse – like a tax inspector, thought Andy. 'What are you going to do with the money?' he asked now.

'We haven't decided yet, but I have an idea. You know that corner of land for sale beyond the walled garden. The bit which used to be an orchard. I thought we might buy it and call it "Kelly's land",' suggested Dad.

'But it's not much more than an acre,' said Emma.

'I thought we could make a way through and turn it into an all-weather school, then the kids can get on with their riding and if Rosie really wants to run a riding school later, it will be there ready,' Dad said.

Rosie was too surprised to speak. She had never imagined her father taking her ambition seriously, now he was talking as though one day it might happen, that she would leave school and become qualified as an instructor – have her own riding school and be able to take in miserable ill-treated ponies. She crossed the kitchen and kissed her father saying, 'Thank you Dad.'

'It's only a suggestion. What do you think?' asked Dad hastily, looking at everyone.

'Land is a good investment. You might get planning permission sometime in the future and then you could make a packet,' said Emma's father.

'It would be lovely for me. I could put up a

116

dressage arena, couldn't I? And you could offer it to the Pony Club for small specialised rallies,' suggested Emma, smiling tentatively.

'And we could give pony rides in it,' said Andy, 'and later on demonstrations of bareback riding, and jousting, that sort of thing. It could be an asset, Dad. As long as it's called "Kelly's land". We must remember Kelly.'

Clara said nothing, not daring to express her thoughts which had been of holidays on sun-drenched beaches, of visits to Paris, Rome or New York.

'Of course there will be something left for each of you – a hundred pounds at least. I shall see to that,' Dad said, looking at Clara. 'It won't all go on Kelly's land.'

'We ought to keep a little in reserve,' said Mum, topping up their glasses with home-made mulberry wine. 'So that there's something in the bank for a rainy day.'

'Yes, we will, love. The land will cost about three thousand. We can do some of the work on it our-selves; that way we will have over a thousand left,' Dad said. Rosie turned away, deciding that she hated money, because whatever she did there would never be enough to rescue all the ponies going for meat, for all the ill-treated ones, for the foals without mothers, for the old and the lame, because she would need hundreds and hundreds of acres and rows and rows of loose boxes to save them all.

'I think I will go out again,' she cried, putting on her coat. 'I want to look at the hedge. I still can't believe I jumped it. And the ponies should be out now; it's too lovely for them to be in a moment longer.'

Andy followed her, saying, 'I never thought it would be like this again. I thought the snow would never end.'

'It could come back,' said Rosie, leading out Lapwing, then watching him roll over and over before going back for Bramble. 'We'll be able to ride tomorrow; the roads must be clear by then,' she said.

Large nearly knocked them over when they led her out of her box. Little rolled over and over so that they wondered whether he would ever stop. Then Emma turned out Sandpiper.

'I'm glad it's over,' she said. 'The snowdrops are coming out and soon there will be crocuses. It feels like spring already.'

'What about your stepmother?' asked Rosie.

'No good. Gone back. Too young. I hated her,' Emma said.

Then they saw that the drive to the house was filling up with cars. 'It's the reporters,' Andy said. 'I'm going to be one when I'm grown up.'

'Why don't you send them away?' asked Emma. 'I would.'

'We can't. It's good for business. After all the beast has made the national dailies,' said Andy.

118

'I don't want to see them. I'm going to hide,' said Rosie. 'But first I'm going to look at the hedge again.'

So they walked across the wet meadows to the hedge which was as high as Rosie, which meant it was a metre and a half high. 'And he jumped it out of snow,' Rosie remembered in wonder. 'But I did fall off. I couldn't help it because he fell down.'

She has said the same thing half a dozen times already, thought Andy. 'She'll tell her grand-children about it. It'll become a legend,' he whispered to Emma, who said, 'Personally I don't want to have any children. I don't intend to marry. I'm going to be single. I'm going to have a career; hopefully I'm going to be a vet, but I shan't allow twitches.'

'But Bert Hayman saved Large's life,' retorted Andy.

And now they could hear Dad calling. 'Come in, all of you. You are wanted. Hurry. Run.'

And the sun was in their eyes as they ran, and the sky suddenly full of dancing clouds.

Later that day Kelly returned home. They had put a notice over the back door saying, WELCOME HOME KELLY. Still drowsy from the anaesthetic he did not see it. They put him to bed and Rosie wept because his shoulder still looked terrible and his eyes were swollen and his jaw misshapen.

'He'll never be the same again, poor Kelly. And he was so brave,' she wept.

'Give him time,' said Mum, putting a blanket tenderly over him.

'The last week has been a very long one; the longest of my life,' Andy said.

The reporters had gone; their tapes used up. Dad started the car and went to the shops to stock up with food. Mum had to milk Marigold so Rosie sat watching Kelly, and looking round she imagined how it must have been in the olden days, with no telephone, no electricity and no vet. People called them the good old days, but now she knew that was not true, for without modern surgery Kelly would surely be dead, and they had hated existing without lights or telephone.

'Poor puma,' exclaimed Clara, looking out of the window some time later. 'Will the police ever know where she came from?'

'I doubt it; the owner is hardly likely to come forward,' replied Dad.

'So we won't get any money for poor Tansy?' asked Andy.

'I think not, though I will have to look at my insurance policy.'

'How can anyone behave like that?' asked Rosie. 'If I had lost my pet puma, I would be searching everywhere.'

'Not if she had done hundreds of pounds worth of damage, and become wild.'

120

'I still think it's wrong.'

'Of course it's wrong,' cried Bronwen. 'And the farmers were involved in the cover-up too, because their animals were covered by insurance against dogs killing their stock, but not against anything else. For all we know, one slipped up here and took a picture of Kelly. I would not put it past them. After all, they had to convince insurance companies. They needed all the evidence they could get, particularly with the media talking about beasts and monsters.'

You mean the people who wanted to kill Kelly, but didn't,' asked Andy.

'Exactly.'

'But in the end he was the hero,' said Rosie, bending over Kelly. 'And no one can take that away from him, can they? The other hero, of course, is Lapwing.'

And the rest of the family, sighing loudly, said, 'Not that again. Please not that again.'

'You can take up cross-country on the strength of it,' Mum said.

'Yes, we'll make a course round our fields,' Dad promised. 'We'll aim for the top.'

'For Badminton,' Andy agreed happily.

'I'll wait until it happens,' Rosie said, knowing that she had changed, that she no longer believed in people as she had before. For had not everyone accused Kelly, she thought, who was blameless, who most likely had been looking for the beast every time he had gone out at night.

The animals had behaved better than the humans, she decided. She knew now that Mum could make mistakes, and that people were still saying 'There's no room at the inn.' So not much had changed in thousands of years.

Then she thought of the outdoor school which might soon be built, and she saw herself standing in the middle, shouting, 'Trot on,' to a class of riders and she was filled with a great upsurge of joy.

Andy was thinking, we've won through. We're stronger because of what has happened. I shall not make the same mistakes again – I will never risk my life again in a blizzard. Meanwhile Clara was wondering whether to spend her hundred pounds on clothes or on a holiday, because it would never cover both. Then Dad called, 'Come into the sitting room. Hurry. You're on television.' And as they rushed through the kitchen Kelly, who was lying in his bed by the Raeburn, raised his head and, looking at them, wagged his extraordinary tail. And that was the best thing of all.

PONIES IN THE FOREST

Christine Pullein-Thompson

Rosie, Clara and Andy help their parents run the Park Farm animal centre. Thinking they need extra help, their father recruits Silas, a boy from the local remand home, to help with the gardening. Silas is quiet and hard-working, but the children don't trust him, even though he is good with the animals, especially the horses. And then something so terrible happens they can hardly bear it, and it seems as if Silas has appeared in his true colours at last. Or has he? This exciting adventure story is a sequel to PONIES IN THE PARK and will be enjoyed by all animal lovers.

THE HORSE AND PONY QUIZ BOOK

Sandy Ransford

How do you pick up a horse's feet? Which breed of horse is thought to be the oldest in the world? In which Olympic Games did Princess Anne ride?

See how much you know about the world of horses and ponies by trying out some of the quizzes in this book. There are questions about feeding, grooming and stable management, breeds, colours and markings, riding, showing and jumping and dozens more subjects. A must for horse and pony lovers of all ages.

BLACK BEAUTY'S FAMILY 1

Diana and Christine Pullein-Thompson

Here are two stories about Black Beauty's relations. Black Romany, three generations before Black Beauty, was a well-bred horse who lived at Belvoir Castle. He hunted with Prince Albert and had lots of exciting adventures trekking across England. Blossom, six generations later, was not so lucky. The product of an unfortunate alliance, she had a life of drudgery working as a cart-horse, and her future seemed bleak until, out of the blue, came unexpected success.

BUYING AND CARING FOR YOUR HORSE AND PONY

Robert Owen and John Bullock

Here, in question and answer form, is all the guidance you'll need when you decide to own a horse or pony. Starting with making the right choice of animal for your own needs, the book goes on to tell you about breeds, stabling, ponies at grass, health, feeding, tack and equipment. At the end are notes on useful organisations such as the Pony Club, and a glossary of horsy terms. There are photographs and drawings throughout and altogether the book will be invaluable for the new young pony owner, as well as giving excellent advice to the more experienced.

PONIES IN THE PARK

Christine Pullein-Thompson

When Andy, Rosie, Clara and their mother are left Park Farm by an elderly uncle, Rosie thinks her dreams have come true. They can live in the country, and have ponies, and learn to ride! But the farm has to pay its way, and their efforts to turn it into an animal centre, with different breeds of ponies and other tourist attractions, are fraught with all kinds of problems. Somehow they must make it work, but can they do it in time? All animal lovers will thoroughly enjoy this exciting adventure story.

If you're an eager Beaver reader, perhaps you ought to try some more of our exciting titles. They are available in bookshops or they can be ordered directly from us. Just complete the form below and enclose the right amount of money and the books will be sent to you at home.

THE SUMMER OF THE WAREHOUSE	Sally Bicknell	£1.25	☐
THE GOOSEBERRY	Joan Lingard	£1.25	☐
PONIES IN THE PARK	Christine Pullein-Thompson	95p	☐
SAVE THE HORSES!	Alexa Romanes	£1.00	☐
THE BUGBEAR	Catherine Storr	95p	☐
WHITE FANG	Jack London	£1.25	☐
GHOSTLY AND GHASTLY	Barbara Ireson, Ed	£1.25	☐
MY FAVOURITE ESCAPE STORIES	P. R. Reid, Ed	95p	☐
THE BEAVER BOOK OF REVOLTING RHYMES	Jennifer and Graeme Curry, Ed	£1.00	☐
RHYME TIME and RHYME TIME 2	Barbara Ireson, Ed	£1.50	☐

And if you would like to hear more about Beaver Books, and find out all the latest news, don't forget the BEAVER BULLETIN. If you just send a stamped self-addressed envelope to Beaver Books, 17-21 Conway Street, LONDON W1P 6JD, we will send you one.

If you would like to order books, please send this form, and the money due to:

HAMLYN PAPERBACK CASH SALES, PO BOX 11, FALMOUTH, CORNWALL, TR10 9EN.

Send a cheque or postal order, and don't forget to include postage at the following rates: UK: 45p for the first book, 20p for second, 14p thereafter to a maximum of £1.63; BFPO and Eire: 45p for first book, 20p for second, 14p per copy for next 7 books, 8p per book thereafter; Overseas: 75p for first book, 21p thereafter.

NAME..

ADDRESS..

....

PLEASE PRINT CLEARLY